Gasoline Cowboy

Gasoline Cowboy

WILLIAM CAMPBELL GAULT

E. P. DUTTON & CO., INC. NEW YORK

F
G

LIBRARY OF CONGRESS
CATALOGING IN PUBLICATION DATA

Gault, William Campbell.   Gasoline cowboy.

SUMMARY: Passionate about racing, a youth travels the
National Circuit participating in motorcycle competitions.

[1. Motorcycle racing—Fiction]   I. Title.
PZ7.G233Gas   [Fic]   73-15784   ISBN 0-525-30352-9

Published simultaneously in Canada by Clarke,
Irwin & Company Limited, Toronto and Vancouver

Designed by Meri Shardin
Printed in the U.S.A.
First Edition

For Jill Shirvanian

Chapter One

The third foster home I went to was the Milgrams'. It was the poorest, but it was the best and the last. I'm surprised they took me. As Mrs. Baskerville explained it, I "was getting a little long in the tooth." She used a lot of British expressions. She was kind of classy for that part of Texas. She ran the Home. I was nine when I went to the Milgrams. I was five when I went to the Home.

I didn't go to the Home because my parents died; for all I know they're still alive. The way I heard if from former neighbors, years later, my dad deserted my mother and she couldn't afford to keep me. They'd been married at sixteen; maybe she had other plans.

Only one scene in those first five years still sticks in my memory: the last Christmas I was with my parents. I don't remember them very well, but I remember what they gave me, a cowboy suit, complete with twin holsters and pistols. And I remember the man who must have been my father saying, "He looks like the real thing, a genuine cowboy!"

I've seen some Frederic Remington cowboys since then, and the movies had them wrong, as usual. I still like western pictures, though, the good ones. When you're young, they all look good.

There was only one theater in Alkali Junction, running movies on weekends. About eighty-seven percent of them were Westerns. I always liked the endings, where the hero rides off into the setting sun under that big lonesome sky. Cowboy heroes were loners, mostly, with no real friends except their horses.

I was on the way, at the Home, of becoming a loner, myself. The first two families that sent me back had the same complaint about me; I was a troublemaker.

Mrs. Adelaide Baskerville was a highly virtuous woman, but tact wasn't one of her virtues. She repeated the complaints to me the Saturday morning she called me into her combination office and sewing room to brief me on our third prospect.

"Their name is Milgram," she said. "Perhaps you know them?"

I shook my head.

"They live only three houses away from where you were born," she explained.

I said nothing.

"They're not wealthy," she said.

If they lived in our old neighborhood, I was sure of that. I continued to say nothing.

"You're a competitive lad, Rex Smalley, and a troubled one," she went on, "but *I've* never thought of you as a troublemaker. We've got along rather well, haven't we?"

I nodded.

She studied me sadly. "You're unusually quiet this morning. Is something bothering you?"

"I don't want to go out again and come back," I said.

"I see. Is it the going out or coming back that bothers you?"

"The two together," I said.

"Then there's no problem." She smiled. "This isn't for a week or a month or a year, Rex. The Milgrams want to adopt you."

I stood there, not believing.

"It's true," she said. "They knew you when you were younger and they've seen you around town since. I'm sure you'll get along."

I still couldn't believe anybody wanted me for keeps.

She said quietly, "They have two children of their own. You will try to get along, won't you, Rex?"

"Yes, ma'm," I said.

They came for me in an old Chevrolet pickup truck, all four of them, about two o'clock that afternoon, Mr. and Mrs. Milgram in front and their kids in the box.

Mr. Milgram was tall and tanned and blond, and Mrs. Milgram was short and dark and on the stocky side. But she was sure pretty.

In Mrs. Baskerville's office, Mr. Milgram said, "I'm surprised you don't remember us, Rex. You used to play with our son Jody."

What was there to say? I said nothing.

3

"Jody's ten now and our daughter Lisa's six," he said. "Jody's kind of feisty, like you. We're going to make it, Rex, aren't we?"

I nodded. In *belief*, this time, not in agreement.

Mrs. Baskerville said, "You understand, of course, that there will be a probationary period first, Mr. Milgram. You will be paid by the county as foster parents until the adoption agreement can be consummated."

"No Milgram ever took money from any county," Mr. Milgram said, "and I don't aim to be the first!"

"We'll accept the money," Mrs. Milgram said. "How long should the adoption take?"

"Three months, at the extreme outside," Mrs. Baskerville told her. She sighed, and smiled at all of us. "Well then, it's settled. I'm going to miss you, Rex."

What could I do? I was too old to cry and too young to come up with the right words. "Thank you, ma'm," I said.

We went out under that big weathered sign, HOME FOR THE HOMELESS, and over to the pickup truck.

Mrs. Milgram said, "Jody and Lisa, this is your new brother."

Lisa smiled. Jody looked away.

Mr. Milgram said, "Say hello, Jody!"

"Hello," Jody said, still looking away.

Mrs. Milgram said, "You can ride in the back, Rex, and help keep an eye on Lisa. We don't live far from here."

I climbed into the box and the pickup wheezed into life. We jounced down the gravel driveway and turned south on the highway.

"What grade are you in?" Lisa asked.

"Fourth," I said.

"I'm in first," she said.

I nodded.

"Jody's in fifth," she told me.

"I know," I said.

He turned from inspecting the countryside to look at me. "How'd you know?"

"I've seen you at school," I explained. "I saw the fight you had with Lenny Wilver."

He made a face. "Lenny Wilver! Phooey!"

I said nothing.

"I suppose Lenny's your friend," he said.

I shook my head.

"What's the matter—-you scared to admit it?"

I looked straight at him. "I'm not scared of anything, including you. Mrs. Baskerville told me not to get into trouble, but don't think I'm scared."

"Huh!" he said. "Good excuse!" He went back to his inspection of the scenery.

It wasn't much to look at; we'd had three years of drought. The land was gray and flat and lifeless. Alkali soil and uncertain weather; many a farmer had gone broke in this part of Texas. We clattered through town, past the feed store, the chain grocer, the Alamo Café, the Rialto Theater. The Rialto was showing Monte Brand in *The Sagebrush Kid* today and I was going to miss it. Monte Brand was one of my favorites.

We moved past the business district and turned right on Pelham Way, a narrow dead-end street that served five houses. The Milgrams lived at the end. The house was frame and needed paint. An old Dodge sedan without wheels was on blocks in the side yard; a tire hung from a rope under the black oak that shaded the front yard.

Jody jumped out and went quickly around the house and out of sight. Mr. Milgram came back to help me with my suitcase.

"Jody will cool off," he said.

I nodded.

"Jody's mean!" Lisa said.

Mr. Milgram said quietly, "He's not mean, Lisa. He's unhappy because he couldn't go to the movie this afternoon. We'll go tonight, the whole family."

Lisa smiled. "Me, too?"

"You, too. Come on, Rex, I'll show you your room. You'll share it with Jody."

It was a small room, but there would be only two of us in it. That was better than four in a room at the Home. We each had our own bed and two drawers in the bureau and and our own half of the closet.

When I'd finished putting away my clothes, Mr. Milgram was still standing there. He looked uncomfortable. Finally, he said, "I want you to know we're happy to have you with us, Rex. And Jody will be."

"Thank you," I said, as uncomfortable as he looked.

Then Lisa was in the doorway. "Will you push me in the swing, Daddy? Jody's not around."

"I have to get back to work," he told her.

"I'll push you, Lisa," I said. "Let's go."

I pushed her in the tire swing, that bundle of sunshine, my new sister, smiling Lisa. Boys of nine don't usually like to play with girls of any age, but Lisa was special.

6

When she got tired of that, we went to the backyard to look at the chickens and play with her pet rabbit. Jody was there, feeding the chickens. He ignored us.

He ignored us at supper, too, all of us. We ate early so we could go to see Monte Brand and still get home before Lisa's bedtime. She rode in front with her parents, Jody and I in the box. It was a short and quiet trip.

I could have said something, maybe, but I didn't figure it would do any good. I knew how stubborn he was. In that fight he'd had with Lenny Wilver, Lenny must have knocked him down half a dozen times. But Jody just kept getting up and Lenny finally ran out of gas.

I didn't want to go back to the Home; the Milgrams were my kind of people. My best chance to stay with them was to keep my mouth shut and my ears open.

I don't remember much about the movie that night or the things that happened in the week that followed. I remember the things I heard. Mr. Milgram had worked at three jobs in the last year. He was working as a bartender at the Alamo Café now and hated it. Mrs. Milgram did some sewing and baking for the few families in town who could afford it. Both of them had been born in this county; neither of them had graduated from high school.

Through this week, Jody had a word for me now and then, but none of the words let me hope that we were ever going to be friends. On Sunday, Mrs. Baskerville came to make her first checkup.

The living room window was open and I hid behind the bush below it to hear what was being said.

How was I getting along with the children, Mrs. Baskerville wanted to know.

"Fine, just fine!" Mr. Milgram said.

"Jody's been a problem," Mrs. Milgram said. "He's stubborn. But he's fair. I'm sure he'll come around."

"And does Rex seem happy?"

"Happy as a lark!" Mr. Milgram said.

"He's adjusted very well, everything considered," Mrs. Milgram said. "It seems peculiar to me that anyone would call him a troublemaker. He's very polite."

"I must say the situation sounds promising, except for this friction with Jody," Mrs. Baskerville said.

Mr. Milgram said, "There's been no friction. None at all!"

A pause, and I could guess that Mrs. Baskerville was waiting for Mrs. Milgram's comment on that. Mrs. Milgram said, "There's been no serious friction and there's not going to be any."

"Let's hope not," Mrs. Baskerville said. "Could I see Rex now?"

"I'll get him," Mr. Milgram said.

I was out in front by the time he came to call me. "Mrs. Baskerville's here," he said.

"I know."

"She wants to be sure you're getting along all right. You are, aren't you, Rex?"

"Fine, just fine!" I said.

He looked at me suspiciously for a few seconds and then he smiled. "You've been listening, huh?"

I nodded.

He laughed. "Why not? March in there and give it to her straight, Rex."

She had only two questions for me. Was I happy? I told

her I was. Then, "How are you getting along with Jody?"

"We haven't had a fight," I said, "and I'm not going to start one."

"That's half the battle," she said. "It's not fun for a boy to have to share his room, you know."

"I know," I agreed.

She sighed. "Yes, of course. Who should know better than you?" She stood up. "Well, I have some other charges I must visit. I do hope this is going to work out."

"Smooth as silk," Mr. Milgram said. "Right as rain!"

He wasn't a man to use new words when the old would do. That has to be a criticism, but it's not a complaint. He has his faults, as we all have. Joe Milgram's faults are part of the reason I love him.

That night, as we were getting ready for bed, Jody asked me, "What did Mrs. Baskerville want?"

"Nothing. She was just checking."

"Checking what?"

"I don't know."

"Don't lie! You know!"

"She was checking me."

"For what?"

"To see if I'm getting along."

"What does that mean?"

"It means I'll probably go back to the Home. And then you can have your room all to yourself again."

He stared at me. "You sure talk foolish!"

I said nothing.

"What do I care about this dumb room?" he asked.

I shrugged.

"You sure talk foolish," he repeated. "Boy!"

"Okay, I talk foolish. I'm not going to argue, Jody. I'm not supposed to argue."

"Why not? You're not in the Home now."

"Not yet," I said. "Good night. Are you going to turn off the light or should I?"

"Do what you want. I don't care what *you* do!"

I had a feeling that was only partly true. I turned out the light and went to bed, another step further from the Home.

Chapter Two

The glacier melted a little more next morning. Jody walked to school with Lisa and me. All last week, he'd gone on ahead of us. He didn't talk much, and I began to wonder if walking with us had been his parents' idea and not his.

But about a block from school, he asked, "You're not really going back to the Home, are you?"

"Not unless I get into trouble."

"Why should you get into trouble?"

I shrugged.

"You sure don't talk much."

"I talk enough. I don't talk to you because you don't talk to me. Ask Lisa how much I talk."

"What does she know? She's only six."

"He talks," Lisa said. "He's not mean, like you, Jody."

"Phooey!" he said.

I said, "If I talk too much, I might get what Lenny Wilver got."

He laughed, another milestone. "He thought he had me, didn't he?"

"He did," I said, "until he ran out of gas."

"Right!" He laughed again. "Right! Oh, boy!"

"I don't run out of gas," I said.

He smiled. "Someday we'll find out. See you later."

We were half a block from school now and he went on ahead. I could understand that. It's all right for a fifth grader to walk to school with a first grader and a fourth grader—but not where his friends can watch him.

Someday we'll find out. . . . The showdown in the dusty street in front of the saloon, the two fastest guns in the West. . . .

The ice continued to thaw. I didn't become Jody's best friend overnight, and never in Texas. He had his own friends there, but he let me tag along. Most kids don't get kinder treatment than that from their real older brothers.

In California, it was different. In California, we met the same people at the same time, together.

California was Mr. Milgram's idea, and it didn't meet with family approval in the beginning. The first time I heard him mention it, Mrs. Milgram asked, "What can we do in California that we can't do here?"

"Eat oranges off the trees and look at movie stars," he said.

"I meant for a living, Joe. What can we do for a living?"

"Living? Do you think standing in a cheap bar listening to loud men argue is living?"

"We eat," she said. "We've saved a few dollars."

"We'll eat. We've never gone hungry."

"The children are happy here," she said. "They have their friends."

"They can make new friends. They're happy here because they've never seen anything better."

She shook her head. "I don't like it, Joe. I just don't like the idea."

Jody was in seventh grade, then, and I was in sixth. A month later, Mr. Milgram quit his job at the Alamo Café and tried selling correspondence courses to the ranchers in the county. Four months later, he was back behind the bar at the Alamo. I don't think it was the loud men arguing that bothered him the most. He simply didn't like to be tied to a time clock. Who does?

He was handy around machines, but so were his friends and neighbors. The one-man garage he'd opened had lasted less than a summer, Jody told me.

Mrs. Milgram was the balance wheel in that family. She made most of the decisions; her earnings kept us going through her husband's job changes.

On the California question, though, she was up against a determined man. Joe Milgram had decided there was no future for him in his home state. He must have known there were better places to live in Texas. He never considered any of them.

He had a persuasive way with him but he was trying to convince a stubborn woman. So he stayed stubborn, too. It was almost a year later, it was summer vacation when he won his wife over.

The furniture wasn't worth moving; they sold it. The

house was rented, so there was no problem there. Transportation was the big problem; that old pickup truck was getting ready to die. Mr. Milgram scouted the county for a week before he found what he wanted, a two-year-old Ford pickup with the 289-inch engine.

He worked on it for another week before we packed the utensils, the linens, and the dishes one hot July morning for our migration to the promising land.

We were all packed and ready to go by nine o'clock. All of us but Mrs. Milgram were in the truck. She stood there, looking at the house and yard. It had never been theirs but it had sheltered them for most of their married life.

"Let's go, Jill," Mr. Milgram called. "I want to make Fort Stockton before dark."

She came over to get into the cab. "That's a long way from here," she said.

"Everything's a long way from here," he told her.

In the box, Jody looked unhappy. It would pass. He had been both happy and unhappy since the decision had been announced to us. Mixed emotions is what it's called, I guess.

We went through town, past the Alamo and the Rialto, past Mrs. Adelaide Baskerville's Home for the Homeless. I had gone to say good-bye to her yesterday and she had cried. Women cry a lot.

We were almost to Laredo and Jody hadn't talked.

"California, here we come!" I said.

He took a deep breath. "Do you think we'll like it, Rex?"

"Why not? What's so great about Alkali Junction?"

He didn't answer. He stared out at the countryside, as he

had that first time I had shared the box of a pickup truck with him. A moody guy, Jody Milgram.

We made Fort Stockton that day, but not before dark. It was close to ten o'clock before we found motel rooms we could afford.

We were up and on the road again early next morning. We had breakfast in El Paso. The taste of pancakes was still in my mouth when I left the state of Texas for the first time in my life, crossing over into New Mexico.

There wasn't much of New Mexico to go through; we spent our second night on the road in Wickenburg, Arizona. It was the first time I had seen the real desert. It looked even more dead than the country around Alkali Junction.

July is the wrong month to be traveling in the desert. We went to bed early that night and were up again while it was still dark. Mr. Milgram wanted most of the desert behind us before that blazing sun could start melting the marrow in our bones.

It came up over the rim of the horizon behind us as we came within sight of Blythe. Blythe was green and looked cool on the far side of the Colorado River from us. It was like a mirage in those desert pictures we'd seen at the Rialto. Blythe is in California; *we* were in California a minute later.

We had to stop for a fruit and vegetable check at the border station, and Mr. Milgram got out to stretch.

"Well, boys, we made it, didn't we? We got through the desert before that sun could get out of bed."

"I guess," Jody said.

"It sure looks like it," I said. "This can't be desert."

15

It was desert; it was an oasis, probably. Because the green was behind us as soon as we left town and the gray, baking sand was all around us again.

"There won't be much of this left," Jody said. "California isn't fat, like Texas. It's long and skinny and we're going the skinny way."

He was right. We were coming into Riverside, the desert behind us, before the sun was much higher in the sky. We didn't even slow down for Riverside; Los Angeles was our goal.

Los Angeles is a big town and a busy town. Most newcomers go there first, because it's the logical place to look for a job in California.

It wasn't for us. We couldn't breathe the air, we couldn't get used to the hustle and the noise. It was cleaner and quieter in the suburbs along the coast, but that was too expensive for us.

Hardin was where we wound up. It wasn't the best part of California. We hadn't come from the best part of Texas. It was a lot nicer than Alkali Junction, I thought. So did Jody and Lisa and Mr. Milgram.

"But what can you do here?" Mrs. Milgram asked her husband. "There can't be many jobs in a town of twenty thousand people."

"Don't worry about me," he told her. "I can always find work. The town is loaded with filling stations. One of them must need a tune-up mechanic."

"Don't you think you should find a job *before* we decide where we're going to live?"

"I like it here," he said. "Trust me, Jill."

It was a time he needed her confidence and she must have realized that. "All right," she agreed. "I have to admit you've never been out of work for long."

He found a job at a filling station two days later, but not as a mechanic. He worked the drive, picked up and delivered customers' cars. He earned less per hour at the station than he had at the Alamo Café, but he worked longer hours here.

The day after he was hired, we went house hunting and found a three-bedroom stucco cottage at the south end of town at a rent Mrs. Milgram decided we could afford. We were now residents of Hardin, California.

At the north end of town was a place we hadn't even noticed, a park surrounded by a high board fence, a park called Tucker's Grove.

There wasn't much grove left in the park, a few eucalypti, maybe half a dozen live oaks. Most of it was taken up by a track, one-third of a mile of banked dirt. It had been a prosperous track when midget racing was popular; the new owner had converted it to motorcycles.

Jody and I were baseball fans at the time; we took more interest in the California Angels, who played twenty miles away, in Anaheim.

Another thing happened that week that is still strong in my memory. Mr. Milgram had gone out early to work on the pickup and Mrs. Milgram asked me to call him for breakfast.

He was in the garage, bending over the engine, I remember, changing a spark plug, when I said, "Time to eat, Mr. Milgram."

17

"Right," he said.

I started to leave the garage and he said, "Just a second, Rex."

I turned around. He was standing straight, now, the new plug in his hand. "It's been almost three years," he said.

I said nothing, not understanding.

"Almost three years you've been with us," he went on. "Can't we think of something better to call me than Mr. Milgram?"

"I guess."

"I've got a feeling you don't want to call me Dad, but how about Joe? I'm not so old and it might make me feel even younger."

"Okay," I said. "Do you think Jody would mind?"

"Not for a minute." He looked at the plug in his hand, at the open garage door behind me, and back at me. "Now, about Mrs. Milgram, I have a feeling there, too—plus some inside information. I think she'd like for you to call her Mom. In fact, I know she would. Could you do that?"

"Sure," I said. "It's been kind of dumb for me, not knowing what to call you and Mrs. Milgram."

He nodded. "We had our own ideas about it, but we didn't want to crowd you. Let me say this, too, while my mouth is warmed up—it's worked out fine, hasn't it?"

"It has for me," I said. 'It's the best home I've ever had."

That morning had meaning for me, but maybe not for you. I put it in because it happened.

Acclimatization is what my seventh-grade English teacher called it. That means getting adjusted to a new background. It didn't take us long to adjust to California. Mom came around to our way of thinking when her flower bed began to blossom. It had been an uphill road, trying to grow flowers in the soil around Alkali Junction.

Two months after Joe went to work at the filling station, their tune-up man decided he might like Hawaii better. So Joe moved up to higher pay, though he still put in a lot of hours.

He didn't work *all* the time. We saw some Angel games and went to Disneyland. Jody got a paper route and I helped him with it, saving our money for bicycles.

It was bicycles first and then cycles for Jody and me. We never really fell in love with the automobile, like most American kids.

Joe had a theory on that. "You're cowboys," he said, "both of you. You've got to have that saddle under you. That's the real evolution of it."

"Evolution of what?" Jody asked.

"Of the horse. Some of these book writers seem to think the automobile replaced the horse, but they're wrong. It replaced the *horse and buggy*. They were for ranchers and lawyers and storekeepers and doctors and bankers. But the saddle horse evolved into the motorcycle, just like the truck replaced the horse and wagon."

"Monte Brand's a cowboy," I pointed out, "and he drives a Rolls Royce and a Ferrari."

"Monte Brand," Joe said firmly, "is not a cowboy. He's an actor, and not a very good one, I'm beginning to realize."

This was sacrilege, but we didn't argue. Joe had been right before.

I was a sophomore in high school and Jody was a junior before we saw our first motorcycle race at Tucker's Grove. Joe's boss had some complimentary tickets he couldn't use and Mom had a garden club meeting that night, so the three of us went. Mom took Lisa to the meeting with her.

I don't remember much about the races that night except that I liked them. I don't even remember the name of the rider who won the feature. It was a chase to me, the classic western chase, all those riders chasing the man in front, who had to be the hero, running away from the misinformed posse.

Joe and Jody had a more technical view of it, which they discussed on the way home: which rider had the best sounding mount and which the best technique, stuff like that.

What I remember about the feature was that nobody caught the man in front. He was out there all alone.

Chapter Three

There were about a dozen older boys at Hardin High School who had motorcycles. Jody and I took more interest in them after we'd seen the race at Tucker's Grove. In the cycles, I mean, not the riders. They called themselves the Hardin Helmets, a rough crew. In a western movie, I figured, they would have been the guys in the black hats.

During the lunch hour at school Monday, Jody and I were studying a little yellow cycle parked at the side of the gym when the owner came along, a senior named Carl Rowland.

"What you looking at, punk?" he asked Jody.

"It says Kawasaki on the tank," Jody answered, "so I guess that's what I'm looking at, a little old one-lung Kawasaki."

"You're a smart kid, aren't you?"

"Smart enough to read a name on a tank," Jody told him.

He stared at Rowland and Rowland stared back and there was one of those silences. Rowland was almost a head taller than Jody, but only about half as wide.

"Let's go, Jody," I said.

"Where?" he asked.

Rowland laughed. "Your buddy's scared. He's not going to back you."

"Of you?" I said. "Scared of *you*? Don't make me laugh!"

He made his move then, reaching out to grab me by the shoulder with his left hand as he drew back his right fist.

I used only one hand, my right. I put it into his stomach with all my might and he folded like a tent pole in a hurricane, bending double, coughing and fighting for breath.

Jody was laughing as we we walked away, but I wasn't. I hate fights. I like contests, but I hate fights. There are times when you have to fight.

"Oh, boy!" Jody said. "It's a good thing Mrs. Baskerville wasn't around."

"I'm in trouble," I said. "Those Helmets stick together."

"I'm not worried."

"You didn't hit him."

"It doesn't matter," Jody said. "If you're in trouble, I'm in trouble. We're brothers, aren't we?"

It was the first time Jody had ever called me that.

Nothing happened that day and I thought (or wanted to think) that maybe Rowland wouldn't mention to his senior friends that he had lost a one-punch fight to a sophomore.

But the next morning, as we were locking our bikes in

the bike stand before school, Rowland was standing next to the motorcycle rack nearby with two other riders.

"That's them," I heard him say.

"We're in for it," I whispered to Jody.

"Phooey!" he said, but his voice was tight.

"Wise guys!" I heard Rowland say. "Are they going to get away with it, Sam?"

"Cool it!" Sam said. "I'll talk to 'em."

He came over alone. I knew who he was, Sam Delgado. He was big and he was dark and he was the boss of the Helmets. He rode a Triumph 500, a real beauty.

He didn't look as if he was hunting trouble. He said calmly, "Hello, fellows."

Jody nodded.

I said, "Hi."

"You had trouble with Carl, yesterday, he tells me."

"A little," Jody said.

"What happened?"

"Rex and I were looking at his cycle and he made some cracks."

"What kind of cracks?"

"He called me a punk and he called Rex yellow. Then he grabbed Rex and Rex hit him in the belly and that was the end of that."

Delgado laughed. "Feisty, aren't you?"

Jody shrugged.

Delgado looked at me. "You hit Carl and he didn't hit you back?"

"I suppose he would have if he could have, but I hit him pretty hard."

23

He laughed again. "Man you are a pair! Where you from?"

"Texas," I said.

He smiled. "Great country, right?"

"Not where we lived," I said.

"I was born in Fort Worth," he told us.

We said nothing.

"Carl," he went on, "has this idea somebody else should do his fighting for him. That's probably why he joined the Helmets. But we're a *club,* not a *gang.* Carl can't seem to get that through his head."

"Maybe he's a slow learner," I suggested.

He nodded. "He won't give you anymore trouble." He looked at our bikes. "Ten speed, huh? Nice!"

"We'll trade you both of them and four hundred dollars for your Triumph," Jody said.

He grinned and shook his head. "No deal. See you." He went back to his friends.

"Maybe they aren't the guys in the black hats," I said.

"What's that supposed to mean?"

"Nothing. Let's go. We're late."

Sam Delgado was more than just the head man of the Helmets. He was the captain of the football team and an all-Citrus-League fullback. His father had come from Italy to Texas and then to California. He'd settled in Citrus Valley, south of town. He had three hundred and twenty acres of orange trees now and enough money to spoil Sam. Except that Sam was a hard guy to spoil.

There was a difference between him and most of the other Helmets. What Sam wanted was excitement; what they wanted was trouble. From my limited experience, a

24

man doesn't need to hunt trouble. Enough of it comes your way in the natural course of life.

It was a low trouble period in the history of the Milgrams. Joe was still working as a mechanic at the same station, Mom was selling enough pies and rolls to keep her flower bed going, and Jody and I were partners in the biggest paper route in town. Lisa was entering a difficult time in any girl's life, but both her parents had enough patience to get her through it.

We saw a lot of races at Tucker's Grove and some AMA National Championship races at Ascot, in Gardena. The real excitement was at Ascot, top riders and top mounts on a track that had been famous since the early days of motor sports.

I don't know which of the three of us loved those races the most, but Joe was the first to buy a cycle.

We had a new Chev pickup by that time, and the cycle was in the box this one afternoon he came home from work. Mom and I were in the front yard, trying to dig the crabgrass out of the dichondra, when he drove in.

She stood up and stared at the cycle, a battered old Harley single. Joe got out of the cab and smiled his prettiest, but Mom said, "Now, what?"

"Now what what?" Joe asked.

"That contraption in the back, that's what."

Joe continued to smile. "We can't afford two cars, can we?"

"Not this week. Why do we need two cars?"

"We don't," he said. "Not anymore. Jill, I'm trying to liberate you."

"Thank you. Let's get back to the original subject."

"We're still on it," he explained. "This eighty-dollar contraption is all I need to get me to work. You can use the Chev everyday. You won't be stuck in the house. You can do the grocery shopping without me, visit your friends—a liberated woman. I did it for you, Jill."

"I'm sure you did," she said. "That was a sweet, eighty-dollar thought, Joe."

"Well," he said, "it might take a few dollars more to get her running again, but nothing that will strain the budget. We are now a one and a half car family."

"And soon," she said, "we will be a three motorcycle and one pickup truck family, the envy of the neighborhood."

"What's for dinner?" Joe asked.

There are guys who went to Harvard who are not as bright as Mom, I'll bet. But she had to wait for her crystal ball award. Because if Joe had a motorcycle, that meant Jody and I did, too. We were young enough and strong enough to pedal our bikes down to the station and borrow it for our paper routes, Jody one day, I the next.

And Joe watched television nights and we didn't, preferring to take turns riding that ancient Harley.

The first time I climbed into the saddle, I knew this was *it,* for me, my kind of machine. I'm not going to bore you with all its advantages over the automobile as transportation; you wouldn't be reading this book if you didn't know that. To me, it was more than transportation, it was the way I wanted to go.

Those were two steps on the troubled road I was to follow, moving to a town that had a racetrack and Joe buying that Harley. They were decisions I hadn't made.

After I climbed into that saddle, the rest of the steps were almost automatic.

Tucker's Grove was not an AMA track; Gus Heinrich, the man who ran the motorcycle racing, had his own rules about engine and rider classification. He had almost the same Junior, Novice, and Expert classes as the AMA, but he had added a few of his own. They weren't designed to give order to the sport; they were designed to increase attendance at his track.

One of his classifications was labeled "Beginners" and it was certainly that, limited to riders who had appeared in competition less than three times, *anywhere*. Mr. Heinrich's office overlooked the parking lot and he had probably noticed how many of his customers came to the races on cycles. If they could be lured onto the track, wouldn't their relatives come (and pay) to watch them compete? This was the class that usually opened his Saturday night card.

One Saturday night, as we were watching this opening chaos, Joe remarked, "I could do better than that."

"Who couldn't?" Jody said.

"Why don't we?" Joe asked.

Jody looked puzzled. "Enter, you mean? Race that old Harley?"

"Why not? She may be old but she's tuned better than most of those clunks."

"Who'd drive?" Jody asked.

"The owner, of course. I hope you boys don't think you have proprietary rights in that machine because you've logged more miles on her than I have."

"We've always accepted you as the owner," Jody said.

27

"But, Pop, you do weigh almost two hundred pounds!"

"You probably weigh a hundred and seventy, yourself. What's an extra thirty pounds to a machine finely tuned by a master mechanic?"

"I only weigh a hundred and forty-seven," I said, "but I hereby waive any claim to consideration."

"Sissy," Jody said.

"Sane," I corrected him. "I'd rather make a U-turn on a freeway in five o'clock traffic than get tangled up in that mess down there."

Jody summed it up for the three of us. "Mom," he said, "would have fits!"

I read somewhere that there's nothing as powerful as an idea whose time has come. The idea of racing in competition had probably been in our minds for some time. Joe's remark during the opening race had only brought it to the surface.

As I've mentioned before, he's a persuasive man and he can stay stubborn when he wants something badly enough. I didn't overhear any of his sales talk, but two weeks later we were entered in the opener at Tucker's Grove.

It was listed as "Beginner Class, Single Cylinder Engines Under 250 cc." in the mimeographed sheet that passed for a program. Our entry read: *Joe Milgram, HD; Rex Smalley, Jody Milgram, pitmen.* I still have that mimeographed sheet.

"Pitmen?" Jody said. "We're big men, tonight. I hope Pop doesn't need any quick emergency service."

I started to answer, but Jody, who was looking over my shoulder, said quietly, "It's that man again."

I turned to see Carl Rowland pushing his little Kawasaki into the next pit. It had been two years since I had hit him in the stomach; I'd avoided him since.

He saw us at the same time. "Well," he said, "the Texas terrors!"

We said nothing. Joe was in the infield, chatting with his boss; Jody and I were alone in the pit.

Rowland looked at the Harley and laughed. "You going to run *that*?"

"We're going to run it," Jody answered. "Looking for trouble, Carl?"

Rowland grinned. "Not tonight. You've got a quick trigger, haven't you?"

Jody stared at him for a second without answering and then went over to the truck to get a can of gasoline.

Rowland shook his head. "Your brother sure holds a grudge, doesn't he? How about you?"

"Only when I lose," I said. "Is this your first race?"

"Third," he said. "First one here. Tonight's the last time I'll be eligible for the easy money. You running in the opener, too?"

"My father is."

He looked at the Harley and smiled. "I wish him luck."

Joe and Jody came back then and a couple of Carl's friends joined him. Both of them had been in the original Hardin Helmets. The club had disbanded this summer, when Sam Delgado had gone on a trip to Italy with his father. I didn't know their names, only their faces.

Joe seemed nervous, tinkering with an engine that didn't need it.

29

Jody winked at me. "You won't get hurt, Pop, if you stay out of the heavy traffic."

"The heavy traffic will soon be behind me," his father informed him. "I could use a little more confidence from my pit crew."

"I'm sure you'll finish," I said. "That's a stubborn machine."

"Thanks, boys. It's plain to me that I have been an overpermissive parent."

The nasal voice on the public address system announced: "And now, fans, for the opening event on this evening's card, Heinrich Enterprises presents ten laps of wild competition between the stars of tomorrow. Fasten your seat belts, folks!"

"And one star of today," Jody added. "Ready, Pop?"

"I'm ready," Joe said. He lifted one long leg over the machine and kicked her into life. "Wish me luck."

"Luck," we said, as he trundled out onto the track, the pie pan with the big "66" on it rattling against the fork. Joe considered 66 his lucky number and it had been open for use.

In the next pit, the Kawasaki chattered into action, following our entry out.

"They'll both be in the last row," Jody said. "That puke had better not crowd Pop."

"Rowland was right," I said. "You sure hold a grudge. Do you still hate Lenny Wilver?"

"I never did. He started it."

Twelve bikes in this curtain raiser, all the machines and all the riders younger than our entry. Chronologically, that is.

Jody must have been sharing my thought. "My three sons," he said.

"What's that mean?"

"That's what Mom calls us, you and me and Pop."

Twelve rasping, whining, clattering machines were shaking the night air now. Carbon monoxide and the acrid smell of burning oil drifted into the pits and over the stands. A beginners' race on a tawdry track, but I could feel my shoulder muscles stiffen in expectation.

"Easy," Jody muttered. "Take it easy, Pop!"

"Don't worry," I said. "He may be young but he's not dumb."

"Yeah. You were right, though, Rex. This was foolish."

"It's a start. We have to start somewhere."

The start was a second away; the green flag was raised. It dropped and twelve unskilled riders on twelve one-cylinder bikes went shrieking into the first turn.

Most of the eyes in the stands, I'm sure, were on the leaders. Jody and I watched the riders in the last row. Joe had the lower track and enough weight to hold his groove into the first turn. The Kawasaki flanking him went high on the bank, losing ground, a light rider on a light machine.

"I think," Jody said, "we have just improved our chances to finish eleventh."

"Maybe even better. Joe's playing it cool."

Jody nodded in agreement. "I expected more fireworks."

Rowland was gunning downtrack now, trying to intimidate Joe. He had as much chance of that as a Volkswagen against a tank; Joe held his line and his lead.

Ahead of him, in the backstretch, a pair of Yamahas and a Honda were playing a game of three-way tag, crowding each other, playing it too close too early. One of them went shooting up the bank of the far turn and we were riding tenth.

"Steady does it," Jody said. "He could win by letting the others lose."

"Not in ten laps," I said. "We're here to learn, not win."

"Yes, grandpa. Here comes our hero!"

Joe swept past the pits, sitting more erectly than the other riders, keeping his weight further back. He had a theory it improved the rear wheel traction. The books I'd read by the experts didn't include this theory, but Joe wasn't a reader.

"He's not running last," Jody said. "That's something. He's too heavy for that bike, though, Rex."

So are you, I thought. I said nothing.

The dust was all around us and the stink of exhaust and the piercing racket of those revving engines, but nobody seemed to mind. Our man was pressing the Honda, his front tire almost rubbing the Honda's rear tire, his weight keeping him below, on the hardest surface of the track. He took the Honda on the turn and rode ninth into the backstretch.

"Hey," Jody said. "Hey!"

"He's making his move," I said.

"Easy," Jody muttered once more. "Take it easy, Pop!"

The Yamaha was within reach now, less than a yard ahead. Joe stayed on the hard ridge and went leaning into the far turn, gaining slowly, but gaining. They were wheel to wheel out of the turn, wheel to wheel past the pits. In the near turn, the Yamaha slid high and we were running eighth.

Jody mumbled something I couldn't hear as Carl Rowland went by in last place, his cycle sputtering.

"I'll settle for eighth, won't you?" Jody asked. "We're not here to prove anything, right? We're here to learn."

"That's what somebody said earlier," I agreed, "but Joe wasn't around to hear it."

Jody sighed and made a face.

"He'll be all right," I said. "He's the sanest man out there."

Jody said nothing, his eyes on his father.

Attrition, I guess it's called. The pair leading the parade had been flirting with disaster since the first lap; they tangled in the ninth and went down together. Joe was still running eighth at the time, almost a lap behind. The collision put him up two notches and that was where he finished, in sixth place.

His face was streaked with dirt when he came in and his goggles spattered with oil. He took off his helmet and asked wearily, "Where'd I finish?"

"Sixth," Jody said. "That's not bad, Pop, for your first try."

He expelled a long breath. "It's a lot harder than it looks. I'm not even sure I enjoy it."

He climbed off and I took the bike.

"It'll get easier," Jody said.

Joe shook his head. "Not at my age."

"It's your decision," Jody said. "I'll be proud to have you in my pit."

"I'd be proud to have both of you in mine," I said.

Chapter Four

Jody and I had sold the paper route that spring and bought a used, Dodge, three-quarter-ton truck. We hauled trash now, mostly the clippings of home gardeners. We were priced below the commercial rate for hauling, so we weren't getting rich, but were earning twice as much as the paper route had paid. We had enough for a pair of cycles.

We were still about six months away from Mom's prophecy, though, having our fun with Joe's machine at Tucker's Grove. Joe's first ride in competition had been his last. Jody was our new cowboy.

I tried to be a good sport about it, an attitude that doesn't come to me as naturally as it should. He was better than Joe, I had to admit. Jody finished fifth in his first race, nosing out creepy Carl Rowland in the last lap. It was a

Novice Class race; once had been too often to appear in that Beginner Class farce.

The cycles were about the same in the Novice Class, the riders not much better. All of the bikes were newer than our Harley; Joe's wrench was what kept us from being shamed in the competition. Add a wrench to that—Jody had inherited his father's touch with machines.

Joe bought his second cycle—a little two-stroke Suzuki Savage—before Jody or I bought our first. It was only a couple years old. The dealer was new and anxious for business, so Joe got a bargain, everything considered. It wasn't his ideal choice; all three of us were yearning for the big-bore jobs. It was simply the best he could afford at the time.

It was a step up, though. Fourth in a Novice sprint was the highest Jody had ever finished before. He took a second in a fifteen-lap finale the first night we raced the Suzuki. We won seventy-five dollars. At our rates, we had to haul a lot of trash to pick up seventy-five dollars.

The good glow of that high finish must have still been with him Friday night. Because he said, "Why don't you try that Novice eight lapper tomorrow night?"

Jody wanted *me* in the saddle? I stared at him.

"You know the track," he said. "You've ridden it plenty of times."

"Not in competition," I pointed out.

"Aren't you the guy who said 'we have to start somewhere'?"

"We started."

"Pop did. I did. And Pop agreed it's your turn now."

Agreed, I thought, *or suggested?* "Okay," I said.

I had ridden on that track plenty of times, as he said. But not on the Suzuki. It would have been better if I'd had more experience with the machine. That sounds like an alibi—and probably is.

There was a field of eighteen riders in the opening sprint for what Gus Heinrich called Novices, that evening of my debut. I knew most of their driving habits, especially their bad ones. Their cycles were no better than ours. Tucker's Grove was a groove track and I knew where the groove was. So the only alibi I had left was lack of practice on the new machine.

It had so much more power than the Harley that I almost went over the guard rail and into the parking lot on the first turn. By the time I could downshift, to get the rear wheel digging again, seventeen machines were in front of me, the nearest a hundred feet away.

The fans were laughing: I was sure Joe and Jody weren't. I gunned downtrack, determined not to embarrass them— or me. Lady Luck helped out in that first lap. The bikes running sixth and seventh collided, careening into the infield through a gap in the fence. I breezed past before they could get back into action.

The rider ahead had a cycle as new as he was. It was really a trail bike, a Suzuki Sierra, but the boys at Tucker's Grove rode what they had and they each had a total of one. So far as I knew, he was the only rider in the race whose experience matched mine (none). With a little more luck, and some skill, I should take him.

I took him on the third lap, inside on the far turn, and squinted through the dust ahead to see who my next victim would be. There was none in sight; I was moving slower than the field.

I twisted a few more revs out of the sweetly singing Suzuki, hoping something I could pass would show up before the checkered flag. My chances of matching Joe's sixth place debut finish or Jody's fifth were slight. But fifteenth in a field of eighteen? That could keep me in the pits forever.

In the fifth lap, a Honda, trailing smoke, went staggering out of action. I was now riding fourteenth. Attrition, which I've mentioned before, had been responsible for three-quarters of my advance. That was no way to go for a man who wanted to go.

I twisted the engine higher and finally found a pigeon in the backstretch on the seventh lap. It was one of Rowland's friends, wheeling a Jawa Trail Boss, a machine designed for enduros.

It certainly wasn't designed for him. He was using all of the track and using it wrong; I went past him when he lost his back wheel in the soft dirt of the north turn.

And that is the story of my first competitive effort, thirteenth in a field of eighteen. When I came into the pit, both Joe and Jody were smiling, but it was purely facial.

"That first turn hurt you," Jody said.

I nodded.

"You played it smart after that, though," Joe added.

Jody slapped my shoulder. "C'mon, Rex, cheer up!"

"There's always next week," Joe said. "Let's get her ready for Jody's heat."

Next week. I hadn't been sentenced to the pits—yet.

Jody finished fifth in his heat, eighth in the feature. That wasn't exactly spectacular, but it was in the upper half of both fields, better than I had done. Maybe, like Carl Rowland, I was a slow learner.

I had some free time Wednesday. Joe let me borrow the Suzuki and Mr. Heinrich let me use the track. For four hours, under a July sun, I searched that surface, seeking the most solid inside and outside routes to the groove, getting the relationship between the machine and the track and my present skill.

Jody was in our room, putting a new plate on his left shoe, when I came home. "How'd it go?" he asked.

"Better—I think."

He smiled. "When we each get our own cycle, you won't be playing second fiddle."

"I don't mind," I lied. "You're our ace—this week."

He continued to smile. "Well, the competition is down to the two of us. Pop's happy in the pit."

"I only compete with myself, Jody," I explained.

"Sure. Natch!"

My second Saturday night showing was an improvement over my first by two places; I finished eleventh. That wasn't shameful, everything considered. But one of the things I considered was how much better Jody had done as a beginner. He hadn't looked that much better riding on the street; he was certainly no more competitive than I was. Why his better record on the track?

There was one obvious conclusion. There were a couple of ways to interpret it. The kindest was that Jody took more chances than I did. The unkind conclusion was that he had more courage.

In all motor sports, there is that decision to be made and its always personal, the thin line that divides the calculated risk from plain recklessness. No men's skills are exactly equal; some men can safely handle higher speeds than others. Winners learn to push their potential right up to the rim of disaster.

My own potential hadn't been extended to either disaster *or* winning; I still had plenty of leeway for experiments, plenty of distance to my goals.

Joe and I were watching Jody one night in a hairy three-bike battle in the lightweight finale when I mentioned this thought I'd had.

"I think Jody's guttier than I am," I said. "I think he has more courage."

Joe shook his head. "Not for one second. He's more belligerent. He enjoys friction. Your courage is a different kind, Rex." He grinned. "A part of it is stubbornness. Over the long run, I wouldn't be surprised if you don't turn out to be more bullheaded than Jody."

Looking back from here, that might have been a good guess. Especially when I think of that stubborn, cold, lonely year when the Number One bug first bit me.

We became a two truck, three motorcycle family that fall, surpassing Mom's prophecy by one Dodge rubbish truck. Jody went big bore with a Honda twin; I stayed under 250 cc. with a Temple Tempest.

It had started as a British firm, but Temple now manufactured most of their cycles in America. Sam Delgado had bought the franchise for the Citrus Valley and he gave me a great deal on a brand new machine.

Sam had tried a season on the AMA Circuit, running a

three-cylinder Temple Tornado without much success. A man needed to be hungrier than Sam would ever get to take the grind and grime, the greasy food and foul weather of all those tank town tracks on the AMA trail.

Rex Smalley and the Temple Tempest—immediate rapport! Like the boy and the girl in those romantic movies, we were made for each other. All the growing doubts I'd had about my chances to become more than an also-ran in competition were gone the first night we rode to battle together. It was an eight-lap Novice race with a field of twenty, and we finished a solid third, less than a hundred feet behind the winner.

Jody and Joe were almost as happy as I was. "Beautiful!" Joe said, "just beautiful!"

"Every move you made was right," Jody said.

"We made 'em together," I explained.

"What?"

"That's the way it was. This machine can read my mind."

Two pits away, Sam Delgado had been visiting with Rowland. He came over to congratulate me and I introduced him to Joe.

"The boys around here have been telling me about your tuning touch, Mr. Milgram," Sam said. "If I ever get solvent, maybe we can do some business."

"You should get solvent with that Temple," Joe said. "I've been working on Rex's and it is one well-engineered motorcycle."

"You and I know it," Sam agreed. "Now the public has to learn it."

The local public got double exposure to Temples that

40

night. Mickey Dorn, another ex-Helmet, had bought a Typhoon from Sam. It was a bike with more sound than fury, but Mickey had enough fury for the combination. He rode like a man who didn't expect to see tomorrow.

Jody was still running Joe's bike in the lightweight sprints and he and Mickey got into a wheel-rubbing duel that had the fans standing for four laps. They tangled in the north turn of the fifth lap and went sliding up the bank together, unhurt, but out of the race.

Jody was fuming when he got back to the pit. "Did you see how he was crowding me?"

I nodded.

Joe smiled. "I would say you were crowding each other."

"A friend of Rowland's," Jody commented. "It figures."

He did better in the big-engine run with his Honda, haunting the leaders all the way, finishing fourth. All in all, it hadn't been a bad night for our team.

We were loading the bikes onto Joe's Chev when Jody said, "A lot of these same guys run at Ascot. Why don't we?"

"Think we're ready?"

"I think we are. Especially now that you've got a cycle that can read your mind. Let's ask the boss."

"I'm good enough for any league," Joe said. "I'm not sure about you two—but we can try it."

I'd had *one* good night at Tucker's Grove. Did that qualify me for the AMA boys at Ascot? Any sensible man would have been doubtful. I wasn't.

I know it sounds kooky to anyone with mechanical sense, but I had a feeling this Tempest had moved me up a class.

Any baling wire and pliers mechanic knows there isn't that much difference between motorcycles—but the optimism persisted, even at Gardena.

Jody was right; some of the Tucker's Grove regulars competed here, along with some AMA names. The difference was that the *cream* of the Tucker's Grove regulars rode at Gardena. There were very few converted trail or street machines the boys could drive to the track; these were pure dirt track cycles, with no brakes.

I would race as a *Provisional* Novice here; the Novice rating had to be earned. Jody was rated a Provisional, too. Jody and I, as a matter of fact, would be competing against each other for the first time. Through the luck of the draw, we were both entered in the five-lap PN opener that Friday night.

We joked about it in the pit. He seemed more confident than I felt, which was natural; he had a better record. He didn't have that hot Tempest, though—I kept telling myself.

"This is a team, remember," Joe warned us. "No duels!"

"Natch," Jody said. "You don't think I'd try to shame my little brother, do you?"

"No duels," Joe repeated.

Mickey Dorn, the man who had hit the dirt with Jody at Tucker's Grove, saw to it that Joe's order was carried out. He was driving for Sam Delgado tonight on a bike exactly like mine. He and Jody flanked each other in the third row at the green flag and they put on a replay of their previous show.

It went over as big here as it had at the Grove, keeping the fans on their feet for three laps. They were within sight of me almost all the way; it was a show I didn't enjoy. Jody was making it too personal, pushing Dorn high on the bank, when it looked to me as if he had the position and plenty of torque to pull away.

The ending was the same. They went down again in the fourth lap. Only some spectacular driving by the riders behind kept it from becoming a mass crackup. Luckily, I was running free and low at the time.

I went past without trouble and finished in seventh place, not bad for a Provisional Novice in his first try at famous Ascot in Gardena.

Chapter Five

Cowboys probably had favorite horses they remembered. Or maybe horses last as long as cowboys; I don't know much about them. That first Temple Tempest, though, that first cycle I owned—I'll *never* forget it.

I raced against better riders on what were supposed to be faster machines, and beat them. A part of that could be credited to Joe's wrench, of course, but not all of it. It was one of those lucky combinations of man and mount that can't be explained sensibly.

I beat Jody for the first time, head to head, in a ten-lap, small-bike finale at Ascot, taking a second to his third. There was some strain in the pit after that one, though Jody smiled and tried to act normally.

When he'd gone out again, for the big-bore feature, Joe

said, "A part of it was trying to adjust to the unexpected, you know."

"Come again?"

"Jody," he explained. "He's *always* finished higher than you have, unless he went down. This time, he didn't and it was nose to nose and—" He shrugged.

"I know," I said. "I understand Jody. He's the same as I am, only bigger."

"Nobody," said Joe, "is exactly the same as anybody else."

Not *exactly* the same, but everybody on that track hated to lose. Not *exactly* the same, or Jody, too, would have traveled the same cold, futile trail toward Number One.

Sam was the man who encouraged me to make that trip. He had Mickey Dorn riding for him, building up local interest in the Temple line. He must have thought I had a greater potential. I'd been winning here and there, at Ventura, Gardena, Sacramento. In the Milgram stable, even Jody was beginning to accept me as a comer.

I was standing next to the hot dog stand at Tucker's Grove one night with Sam when he said, "Treadmill to nowhere."

"What is?"

"All these bush league tracks. There are only about half a dozen men in the country who make a living from motorcycle racing."

"I know. And none of them race here. These boys are here for the fun and games."

"Not you."

"Not me," I agreed.

"When do you make your move?"

I shrugged. "Not now, that's for sure. Maybe never. I suppose you're talking about the National Circuit?"

"What else?"

The AMA sanctioned thousands of races a year but only about two dozen or so earned a rider points toward the Grand National Championship. Traveling from coast to coast to appear in two dozen races a year, that was the National Circuit.

"You earn that Number One," Sam went on, "and you'll make more in endorsements alone than Gus Heinrich pays here in a year."

Number One was the golden number the national AMA champion carried on his cycle. I shook my head, "You're dreaming!"

"Don't tell me you've never thought about it."

"I've thought about it. Even nine-year-old kids with mini-bikes dream about it. But I don't have the money or the moxie for that kind of company, not yet."

"I could get you a little backing from Temple. I could probably get you a big bike to use and free parts. The Tempest you're riding is good enough for the lightweight competition."

"But I'm not. Sam, I've ridden dirt tracks and a couple of desert scrambles. I don't know anything about hardtop tracks or real moto-cross or enduros. I'm still as green as grass!"

"And better than you think." He smiled. "You're probably right; you're not ready, yet. I thought I'd plant the bug. When the time comes, if you need help—"

"I'll think of you," I promised, "the only rich friend I have."

He shook his head. "My pa is rich. I go my own way. Think of me as your friendly, local Temple dealer. You've already sold a couple cycles for me, Texas."

"From also-ran to winner," I said, "all because of Temple!"

He kept a straight face. "That's what I've been telling the prospects—if Rex Smalley can win on a Temple, *anyone* can!"

I'd been lucky. I'd avoided some mass spills by the skin of my teeth and had very little mechanical trouble. I'd also (for the record) gone wheel to wheel with Hud Eggleton for eight laps at Ascot and taken him. Hud had been only seven championship points short of winning Number One last year. So it isn't immodest to say it had been more than luck. It would be arrogant foolishness to think I was ready to win in the kind of company Hud usually kept. The rubbish truck was still my safest economic bet.

It wasn't only the money. I wouldn't have Joe's tuning. He had bought an interest in the station where he worked, so there was no way he'd be able to barnstorm around the country with me.

Our business was less complicated; Jody or I could leave it for a year and afford to hire a man to do the work of the missing partner. But how did I know Jody wasn't dreaming the same foolish dream I was? Both partners couldn't leave.

We had started at Tucker's Grove and gone on to better tracks further from home, none of it at my suggestion, most of it at Jody's. Which meant to me that it hadn't been pure fun and games with him; he, too, was trying to improve, to test himself against better competition, and learn to ride on all surfaces.

47

We had to travel at night, both ways, to squeeze a hundred-miler at Phoenix into a weekend. Jody was entered on the big bike, so our competition wasn't direct. We both took a third in our class.

"That's better," he said in the pit.

"Better than what?"

"Better than I've been doing lately." He paused—and then added, "Against you."

I laughed. "You sure set small goals for yourself."

"I think we both have the same goal, but won't admit it. When did we get secretive, baby brother?"

"I guess you mean we both want to travel the National Circuit?"

He nodded.

"I'm not ready for it," I said. "If you don't mind a frank opinion, neither are you."

"We're both trying to get ready for it, though, aren't we?"

"It looks that way."

"But we can't leave the business, not at the same time."

"I've thought about that. You're the senior partner, Jody."

He frowned. "What's that supposed to mean?"

"You make the decisions. You decide who goes."

He shook his head. "We can both go, Rex, but not the same year."

I nodded and waited. He had more on his mind.

"When we decide we're ready," he went on, "the one who's readiest takes the first year."

"Readiest—?"

"Hottest, winningest—call it what you want. We'll know."

I thought I knew, already, but that could change.

"I think you should start riding my Honda once in a while," he said. "You can't earn enough points on light-weight alone."

"I know. But I've got a feeling Sam Delgado is about ready to let me run a Temple Tornado for him. Dorn hasn't been doing so well."

"Except against me," Jody said. "Let's load the bikes."

Joe couldn't make the trip; we'd had to rely on friendly competitors' pitmen to keep us informed during the race. It hadn't seemed the same without Joe.

My luck held, my communion with the Tempest. Jody was still running two bikes through May. That naturally gave him a total of more high finishes. But Sam came through with a Tornado for me in June and the point race was on. We both had AMA cards now; we invented our own point system for the races at Tucker's Grove.

Joe didn't like it. "We're a team," he told us, "remember that! We're one family."

"It's only a friendly competition, Pop," Jody told him.

"It hasn't looked like that to me lately. You keep it friendly, hear?"

"Natch," Jody said.

"Of course," I said.

"I'm serious," he warned us. "You keep going the way you've been going and both of you can look for a new mechanic."

Friendly competition? The words fight each other. A man can be both a friend and a competitor. To keep the world civilized, he had better be. But it's not a balance easily or naturally achieved.

There was still a lot of loner in me. It was still Rex Smalley against the world. Off the track, I guess I was a good mixer. On the track, I gave no quarter and expected none. That's probably true of any rider who finishes in the top half of his field.

Jody and I see-sawed through the summer. First he was leading and then I. Where he beat me was on the big machine. That Tornado was a lot of motorcycle, but I hadn't mastered the feel of it; the Tempest was more my kind of bike.

We were running the short tracks mostly and that might have been why. At Daytona, or the paved mile tracks, those big and powerful engines came into their own. Where we usually ran, they felt cumbersome and unresponsive.

Joe's warning didn't go unheeded. Jody and I never rubbed tires or tried to shove a wheel inside on the turns when the other had the groove. Joe was a genial father but there was no doubt in our minds about who was the boss.

At San Valdesto, in September, Jody had his best day, a first in the big-bore event, a third in the lightweight. I took a second in the lightweight and wound up against a hay bale, out of the running, in the heavy machine windup.

In the pit, he looked smug. He had come here in the lead and increased his advantage. There were only a few big point events left in the year.

"I wonder if Daytona will be warm?" he said.

"You'll find out in a year or two," I answered. "Are we going to make Phoenix again?"

"If you want to."

"I want to. There's enough track there for that Tornado.

I could pick up some extra points. They're running the different classifications in separate races this time."

"I might have a Honda in both classes," he told me. "I've been talking with Aljanian."

Sarkis Aljanian was a Fullerton Honda dealer. He backed two or three riders in western events every season. I said, "That Suzuki has been good to you. I wouldn't desert her now."

"I want to get used to the Honda," Jody explained. I'll probably be racing her on the National Trail next year. And Pop has decided he needs the Suzuki to get to work."

I said nothing. *Pride,* I thought, *goeth before the fall.*

At Tucker's Grove, a week later, I cut into his point advantage, winning the feature, while he finished out of the money. Tucker's Grove didn't rate many points in our personal count, but I needed to be close enough to make Phoenix the decider. The Tornado and I were beginning to understand each other, and the paved mile at Phoenix was her kind of track.

On the ride home that night, Joe said, "I've got a big wad of vacation time coming. I think I'll take a day or two off to make that Phoenix trip with you boys."

Jody nudged me with his elbow. "Don't you trust us, Pop?"

"I'm beginning to. But I think Rex needs my wrench there more than you do. You wouldn't want an unfair edge, would you?"

"I want any kind of edge I can get," Jody answered. "Even if I don't need it."

At Oxnard, late in the month, I got an unrequested assist

from Mickey Dorn in my point race with Jody. In their few outings Jody had been taking Mickey. To add fuel to an already overheated situation, Mickey's new backer, a local Harley dealer, was at the race to watch his star perform.

They were in the card-opening, big-engine qualifying heat and it was a frightening personal war from the start. Most of the fans gave noisy approval; the men watching from the pits were silent.

"I ought to flag him in," Joe shouted, above the racket.

"He wouldn't come," I answered.

Joe nodded agreement, his face grim. He could have been sorry, right now, that he had ever bought that Harley.

The inevitable happened in the far turn of the last lap. Jody moved higher, going in, to straighten out the corner, and Mickey followed him up. When Jody started down again, Dorn didn't give him clearance.

Somehow, Jody avoided the collision, cutting sharply uptrack. The soft dirt caught his front wheel there and wrenched him out of control. The wheel slammed into the low guardrail; both the bike and Jody went somersaulting over the bank.

There was a shriek from the stands—and a silence. Joe's hand was gripping my shoulder. He muttered something, but I couldn't make out the words.

Then Jody appeared at the rim of the bank, waving to show he was all right. Joe's hand left my shoulder. "That hothead will *never* learn," he said hoarsely.

It not only lost him points in the opener; it kept him out of the big-engine finale. I beat him by two places in the lightweight windup and picked up enough points on the big bike to make Phoenix the decider.

Joe didn't say a word on the trip home. He and Jody had exchanged some harsh words in the pit after the spill. Jody's silence matched his father's. They rarely quarreled; I was uncomfortable, sitting between them.

At home, just before he opened the cab door to get out, Jody said quietly, "I'm sorry, Pop."

Joe nodded, his eyes straight ahead. "It's over and done with. But I'm certainly going to make the Phoenix trip now."

In our room, Jody said, "That Dorn and I are going to tangle one of these days. He hasn't got big Sam Delgado to do his fighting for him anymore."

Nobody had ever been called on to do Mickey's fighting for him. I said nothing.

"Did you see how he pushed me over the bank?"

To me, Mickey had held a perfectly legal line and position. I said, "You scared your dad, Jody. He's bound to worry about you, no matter how old you are."

"We're talking about Dorn," he said, "not Pop!"

I shrugged and said nothing.

"Old quiet Rex," he said. "Old wordless Rex."

I grinned at him. "I talk. Ask Lisa how much I talk."

He shook his head. "Oh, man! What a memory—all the way back to fifth grade!"

"Fourth," I said. "Fourth for me and fifth for you. Cheer up! Maybe Dorn won't be at Phoenix."

Dorn was there, along with his Oxnard backer. And Carl Rowland, temporarily without a mount, was working his pit. Carl came over to shoot the breeze with us.

He didn't bother me. He had progressed from a windy jerk to a windy semijerk, and I considered any man trying

53

to improve worth my time. Jody gave him neither a word nor a glance; Carl got the message and stayed only a few minutes.

"You should talk about *my* memory!" I kidded Jody.

"I don't like him," Jody said. "I don't like him and I don't like Dorn. I don't like any of those ex-Helmets, except maybe Sam Delgado."

Joe sighed. "Just be sure you leave that attitude in the pit."

Jody didn't answer, working over his new four-stroke, 174 cc. Honda that Aljanian had offered him two days ago.

In the first lightweight qualifying heat, Jody didn't come up against Dorn. I did, though. He flanked me in the second row.

He looked over and grinned. "Too bad Jody isn't in this heat."

I said nothing.

"Well, if I take you, I guess that means I would have taken him. You're better than he is on these small bikes."

I made no comment.

"You don't talk much, do you?"

"Not on the track," I told him. "The way I see it, tracks are for racing and lecture halls for talking. Maybe you ought to team up with Carl and go on a lecture tour."

He continued to grin. "Not bad! Prepare to race, Gabby."

The green flag was raised. It dropped, and we were back to the racket and the stink that only a fool could relish. I loved it. The smell of burning oil from the two-strokes, the screech of tires, the reverberating boom of twenty engines blending, the noise of the crowd, it was all here at Phoenix, all but the dust.

54

Dorn was no problem in that sprint, not to me. I left him behind on the first turn and went up to play with the leaders. Hud Eggleton was one of them. I had taken him at Ascot. I had taken him *once*—and competed against him often.

There was another big name rider pacing it out with Hud, Dick Mann, riding a borrowed Suzuki. Dick had won more races than I had seen in my lifetime but age hadn't slowed him down. He and Hud set a pace I knew I couldn't match.

I tailed them, prepared to meet any competition from lesser men coming up behind. The lesser men stayed behind; the names went on to finish one, two, Mann the winner. Yours truly finished third, a respectable finish for a greenie in that field.

"Nice!" Jody said.

"Which means short of spectacular."

"You qualified. Isn't that why you were out there?"

"That's never why I'm out there. I didn't figure I was ready to take Mann *and* Eggleton in the same five-lap race."

"Sound thinking. What were you and Dorn yacking about?"

"About a lecture tour he and Carl are planning. Where did he finish?"

"Sixth. Lecture tour—?"

"It's time to get lined up for your heat. Move, cowboy!"

Though I hadn't mentioned it to him, I thought it had been a mistake for Jody to break in that Honda at a race this important to both of us. He knew all the performance characteristics of the Suzuki; this new bike was still a stranger to him.

55

The mistake had been mine. He and Joe, in two days, had turned that sturdy, street pussy cat into a track tiger. The sense of drift and traction a rider needed on the dirt ovals wasn't needed here; torque was king.

There were four other Hondas in the sprint roughly similar. They were no threat to Jody. He and a local rider on a Harley were a pair of hares before a field of hounds, gaining ground on their pursuers through every lap.

Of course, I told myself, Hud Eggleton and Mann aren't in *this* race. This field, I explained carefully to myself, doesn't look as fast as the one I was in. I didn't need to tell myself anymore than that; the starter's checkered flag told me the important fact. Jody was the winner.

"I'll send you a postcard from Daytona," he promised.

"You looked very sharp out there," I admitted. "The day is not over."

The lightweight windup was a twenty-mile race, open to the upper half finishers of each qualifying heat. Jody was in the third row, I was in the second. I had been right about the speed of his heat.

Based on past performances, this was my best hope for points. I had to pick up enough of them here to overbalance his (temporary) superiority on the heavy bike.

The show featured the same stars as the opening heat, Hud Eggleton and Dick Mann. Hud was determined to prove no rider could beat him twice on the same day, an opinion not shared by Mann. They had their private war; the trailing field fought it out to determine who would be king of the also-rans.

Halfway through the race, Joe's board informed me I was riding fifth. Both of the bikes between me and the leading pair were in sight and neither one was Jody's. I had to be in front of him. But how far?

The bike directly behind me was a Kawasaki, the bikes behind that too far back to identify. I would have to beat Jody by more than one or two places to earn the points I needed.

I didn't do it, taking a fourth to his sixth. The heavy-weight competition coming up would decide who would make the trip. Jody had a big edge—at the moment.

Hud Eggleton, who had won the race, came over to the pit before the first heavyweight heat to study my bikes.

"Sam Delgado's been talking them up to me for a month," he explained. "How do you like 'em?"

"I've done all right on the Tempest," I said. "That Tornado's still too much machine for me."

"As he will soon prove to one and all," Jody said.

Hud smiled, looking between us. "Family war?"

"Friendly competition," Jody said. "Who's going to be Number One this year?"

Hud shrugged. "It's still wide open. Last year cured me. I thought I had it made—until Sacramento."

He had cracked up at Sacramento. He hadn't competed in any eastern championship races this year.

"You only missed it by seven points!" Jody said.

"And one broken arm and two concussions and a torn cartilage." Hud shook his head. "That's a rough, cold trail. I'll stay in the West and play in the sun. There are better ways of making a living."

Surer, I thought, *but not better.*

Hud smiled, as though he had read my mind. "But it's a thing a man has to find out for himself. Luck, boys."

The word he left us with was the word that described that day of decision; it was pure luck. The luck was bad and it was Jody's.

Our heats were reversed this time; he drew the fast field. There were three riders high in combined points in his heat, all of them still within reach of a top twenty ranking. They all beat him, and so did Mickey Dorn. He finished fifth.

Eggleton had confined his competition to lightweight this afternoon. The only ace in my heat was Dick Mann on another borrowed bike. The bike wasn't as durable as Mann. It conked out in the first lap. It was now a nonstar race between peers and every rider in it probably thought he had a chance for the top spot.

The same local boy who had dueled with Jody in the lightweight heat rode a bigger Harley to victory in this one, nosing me out by less than a foot. I was disappointed, though I had no right to be. It was the highest I had ever finished on the big machine.

The climax of that day should have been the heavyweight finale. Jody and I were almost even in points; this afternoon's windup would decide who would make the big trip next year. It would be exciting to report a screaming duel between us. It wouldn't be true. He cracked a piston in the third lap; I coasted to a sixth-place finish.

Nobody of Jody's temperament could be a good loser, but he tried.

"Send me a postcard from Daytona," he said.

Chapter Six

We stopped in Wickenburg to eat on the way home. "Remember when we stayed here?" Joe asked.

Jody nodded.

I said, "I remember it was hot and we went to bed early so we could get up in time to beat the sun across the desert."

Joe sighed. "It's worked out all right, hasn't it?"

"Until today," Jody said.

Joe and I laughed. My laugh was embarrassed. I knew Jody; I could feel for him. We shared a lot of attitudes. Empathy's the word.

In a thirty-bike field, there have to be twenty-nine losers. That certainly gave all of us a lot of practice at losing. With that much practice, why couldn't we learn to be good at it?

There were still two short-track events left in the California season, races that we hadn't included in our point count. One was at Padre, the other in Silas. They were too cramped for the big bikes; I competed on the Tempest, Jody on his new Honda.

I took a second in the feature at Padre, Jody a fourth. He won at Silas, I finished eighth, after a spill.

"We should have included these last two races," he said, smiling.

I said nothing.

"A joke, son," Jody explained. "A little, dumb joke."

"Yes, partner. You were joking, *almost*. If you'd rather go the first year, it's okay with me."

"You're going," he said, "and you're going to make us proud."

The masculine majority in our family could understand why I wanted to go; the feminine minority held a different view.

"A year?" Mom said. "A whole year away from us?"

"Almost. Unless I get hungry before then, unless I don't win any money."

"It's crazy," Lisa said, "just crazy!"

I didn't argue with her. She was probably right.

"Those noisy, wild machines," Mom asked, "are they going to be your whole life?"

"I hope so. If I'm good enough."

"There's no point in talking about it," she said. "I don't understand it and there's no way you could make me understand it. You're old enough now to know your own mind."

Pleasing Mom was important to me. She was a sensible woman and tolerant of masculine foolishness, but she had called it right. There was no way I could make her understand why a man would go hungry and risk disaster for the childish pleasure of wearing a big number one on the front of his motorcycle.

Sam didn't get too much factory help; most of the money he risked on me was his own. Besides my Tempest, I would take the Tornado I'd been using and a Trail Cat that Jody, Joe, and I had modified for the Tourist Trophy meets. Temple's contribution was extra parts for all three machines.

"If they knew you as well as I do," Sam told me, "I could have weaseled more out of them. Well, maybe next year—"

"Next year, Jody goes," I said. I told him about our agreement.

"That was foolish," he said. "Jody's good, but you're better. He knows that, doesn't he?"

"No," I answered. "And I don't intend to be the one who tells him."

"He isn't a man you can tell things," Sam agreed. "He has to learn everything the hard way."

Who doesn't? Both on and off the track. Pain or expense or both can really rivet a lesson in a man's memory.

Business was good that winter and I saved some money. Jody suggested he could send me the difference each week between my share of the profits and the salary of my substitute, but I turned him down.

"We'll need a new truck this summer and we'll be hiring temporary help in the spring. That'll take all the money we have."

"This *summer*—? I thought you were taking the Dodge on the trip."

I shook my head.

"You buying a truck?"

I shook my head.

He stared at me. "You're getting that quiet, stubborn look again. What goes on, Rex?"

"I'm sharing expenses," I said. "I'm traveling with Carl in his new camper."

"Carl? Carl Rowland? *Carl Rowland!*"

I nodded.

He seemed stunned. "I can't believe it!"

"He's not one of my favorite people," I admitted. "But I like him better than you do. How else can I go? That Dodge would never make it, and I need what money I have for food."

"Carl Rowland!" he said for the fourth time. "He hasn't got it, man, not at that level!"

"I know. I'm sure he does, too. I think he just wants an excuse to travel."

Jody was breathing heavily, staring at the ground. "So that's why he's been hanging around here lately."

That's one of the reasons, I thought. *The other is Lisa.*

They had been dating, keeping it a secret from Jody, knowing his temper. I didn't mention it now for the same reason.

Except for his nonstop mouth and his sarcasm, Carl was almost all right. He was the youngest child of indulgent parents and he hadn't outgrown it. His high school arrogance was gone; he didn't start any fights now that he couldn't win. He had an active sense of humor and a sharp perception of each man's Achilles' heel—two qualities that don't add up to popularity.

There were riders more objectionable than Carl that Jody could tolerate, riders who hadn't given him any *personal* reason to dislike them—yet.

There was some strain between us before I left for Daytona and it made me uncomfortable. I felt disloyal. With Jody, you accepted him all the way, including opinions, or you were disloyal. It was an unfair attitude and I knew it. I still felt disloyal.

The rainy morning that Carl pulled his camper into our driveway, the whole family was out to see me off, including Jody. Carl had a trailer behind the camper.

We loaded the bikes on the trailer and Jody looked at me. "Luck," he said, "luck, brother."

In the finals, in the showdown, Jody always came through. "Thanks," I said. "Get rich while I'm gone and you can go first class next year."

"Sure," he said. "Natch."

Carl smiled at Lisa and Lisa smiled back. Mom kissed me and said, "So long, you crazy kid."

Joe punched my shoulder and said, "Show 'em, champ!"

"I'll do what I can," I promised. "I may be home early."

"Never!" Joe said. "Not in a million years!"

We were about two blocks from the house when Carl said, "Mr. Milgram's not like Jody, is he?"

"In some ways, he is. It takes time to know Jody."

Silence for about three blocks and then Carl laughed. "Weird, huh? You're the guy who hit me but Jody's the guy who hates me."

"If I'd known you were going to buy a camper someday, I never would have hit you, Carl. Let's think about now. Yesterday's dead."

It wasn't a bad trip east. Carl talked and I listened, and the camper purred along. Even those solvent cowboys in the top ten didn't travel any better than this.

There would be almost two dozen stops on the circuit this year where a rider could earn championship points. We didn't intend to make all of them. There would be four Tourist Trophy steeplechase events. Our combined experience in steeplechase racing added up to zero, but we planned to compete in at least two of them.

"Dirt track," Carl said, "that's about all we know."

"Twelve of the races will be dirt track and six of those on half-mile tracks. We ought to know *them* by now."

"In the West. Sam told me it's different in the East. The surface is different and so is the weather. Well, at least we'll get to see the country."

"I didn't come for the scenery," I said.

He laughed. "I guessed that! You are one determined man, aren't you?"

"I'm doing what I want to do and I mean to get good at it."

"Good—or the best?"

"That would be good enough."

Through Arizona and New Mexico, the road unwound, and into Texas. We stayed overnight at a trailer park west of Fort Worth.

"Your old stamping grounds," Carl commented.

"Not around here. Further south."

"To hear Sam talk, you'd think it's the greatest state in the Union."

"Sam was rich."

"Not then, he wasn't."

64

"He was richer than we were. Almost everybody in Texas was richer than we were."

Carl laughed. "I see now what you mean about yesterday being dead. You want to bury it, huh?"

I shrugged.

"You can't bury the past," he said. "It's made you what you are."

"Is that so? And what am I?"

"Aggressive, competitive, ambitious."

"You forgot to add 'short.' "

He laughed again. "That's an add, all right. It makes you *more* aggressive, competitive, and ambitious."

I said nothing.

"Your turn," Carl said.

"At what?"

"How do you see me?"

"A spoiled kid who talks too much. But bright—and sometimes funny."

He smiled. "You win. I'll cook dinner."

I shook my head. "If I won, I'll cook dinner. I can't seem to develop a taste for underdone hamburgers."

"We sophisticates call them rare," he told me. "Make mine rare."

This time, I laughed. "There's only one way to get the last word with you."

"How?"

"Hit you in the belly. Two rare and two cooked hamburgers coming up!"

From Fort Worth to Shreveport, Louisiana, and down into Mississippi, heading east, bearing south. Halfway through Alabama, we swung down toward Florida.

We were about ten miles above Daytona Beach before we had our first view of the Atlantic Ocean. We parked to look at it.

"It's bluer than the Pacific," Carl decided.

"And choppier," I added. "Pacific means peaceful, doesn't it?"

"Right. And Rex means king. Which king where you named after?"

"No king. Joe Milgram told me I was named after Rex Steele."

"Who's Rex Steele?"

"The second fastest gun in the Rialto. A movie star out of the past, the dead, dead past. Let's go."

Carl sighed. "Your favorite two-word sentence—let's go!"

Down the eastern coast we rolled, toward mecca, toward the town that had made itself famous through wheels, the beach that had held all the straightaway wheeled records until the salt flats in Utah had been discovered.

It was no longer a beach strip where men raced against time. The main track had 31 degree banks on its turns and two and a half miles of paved superspeedway, where stock cars traveled above two hundred miles an hour. There was an infield road course almost four miles long for sports cars and motorcycles. There was a huge cafeteria—and a fully equipped hospital.

"The big time," Carl said, as we pulled into the riders' parking area. "The big time and the big boys. Well, I repeat, it was an interesting trip."

"We've seen most of these boys before. They don't scare you, do they?"

"Only on a track. We've never seen them in bunches. They'll *all* be here, you know."

"Including one who swore he wouldn't," I said. "Who's that standing next to the blue van over there?"

"It looks like Hud Eggleton to me."

It was. We parked in the space next to his and went over to get the word. He was trundling a big Triumph out of the van.

"Factory rider," he explained. "That changed my mind. Triumph pays for everything."

"Including concussions, broken arms, and torn cartilages?" I asked.

He nodded, playing it straight. "Harley spends more money, but Triumph's got the winning team this year."

"And what do the poor independents do?" Carl asked.

Hud smiled. "They go back to Tucker's Grove. You boys should have stayed in Hardin."

"We only came for the scenery," Carl said, "but we might as well hang around for the action. I thought you were going to buy a Temple?"

"I did. For the street. That's a nice, soft, comfortable street machine."

Carl laughed. "The arrogance of the mighty! Good luck, Hud. You'll need it."

"Everybody does," Hud said. "C'mon, get your bikes. I'll lead you children through the trail the AMA has set up for us."

I took the Tempest, Carl his new Honda. We had come early; there were only a few riders in the pits and out on the track.

The course was over three miles long, with five turns in

67

the infield, both right and left, before we churned through a mean hairpin and came up onto the main track. Hud threw away the anchor here. He must have been doing 150 mph down the long backstretch and into that big banked curve. He picked up a lot of ground on us. He had called it right. At this speed, we were innocent children.

The most dangerous test was still ahead, downshifting from all out to 50 mph for the narrow corner to the left that led back to the infield. We were lucky that Hud was so far in front by this time; we had enough warning to slow down for the turn.

He waited for us back at the starting line. He was grinning. "Fun?"

"It's a little trickier than Tucker's Grove," Carl admitted. I said nothing.

"You'll need fairings on those bikes," Hud said. "They'll help with the wind up on the main track."

"We brought 'em," Carl said.

"Thanks for the education," I said.

He nodded. "Any time. And Carl—"

"What?"

"Good luck. You'll need it." He waved and gunned out to start the course again.

"Smart Aleck!" Carl said.

Smarter Aleck, I thought. I said, "Let's try it again. We can get in a few more laps before the sun goes down."

"You lead," Carl said. "I'm still shaking. Hud made us look bad, didn't he?"

"He was running the big bike," I pointed out. "That's all Triumph makes. Let's go!"

He followed me for five laps before we called it quits for the day. It was a different world, a different league. It was a long way from Tucker's Grove, a big step up. It was an even bigger step from Alkali Junction.

But I was here.

Chapter Seven

My old Rialto idols were dim in my memory; my new idols were in the cafeteria where we went for dinner: Dick Mann and Gary Nixon, Carroll Resweber, Mark Brelsford, Gene Romero, Bart Markel.

We didn't sit with any of them. We sat with Mickey Dorn.

"Jody should see you now," Carl quipped, "consorting with his enemies."

"You were in the Helmets," I explained.

"So was Sam Delgado," Mickey said. "And now he's backing you."

"How about the others?"

Mickey shrugged. "Who knows? A couple of them are in jail."

"Most of them were creeps," I said. "You know *that*. Jody's kind of old fashioned. He judges a man by the company he keeps."

"In high school?"

"That's where we were at the time. Let's talk about now."

"Now," said Mickey, "I have three bikes in the van and a Harley dealer in Oxnard who thinks I'm a comer. I look around this room and think that maybe the man made a bad investment."

"Don't lose any sleep over it," Carl advised him. "Harley-Davidson is probably picking up three-quarters of the dealer's tab and they have *lots* of money."

"They're not contributing a dime," Mickey told him. "The man's a fan."

"Count your blessings," Carl said. "The manufacturers want winners. This man just wants a hero."

Mickey smiled. "I aim to give him both in one attractive package. But it's not going to be easy."

True, true, true. . . . Luck and skill and a hot machine can combine to win a race. But on those too often days when the combination lacks an element, that old devil money takes over. Money can replace a broken part, get you to the next race, keep you in mechanics and pitmen and hamburgers, keep you going until the combination is right again.

The factory riders had the big money behind them. The privateers had to scratch for their traveling money in the nonchampionship races along the trail, on the dusty, low-purse tracks of the tank towns.

"You're looking gloomy," Mickey said.

"I'm thinking the same thing you are," I told him. "There

71

are too many big names in this room. Let's go back to your motel and watch television."

The kind of motel Mickey could afford didn't have television in the rooms, only in the lobby. It had already been taken over by some senior citizens who were watching a 1940 movie. Carl and I went back to the camper to write letters.

In the morning, we worked on our bikes. After lunch (two hot dogs and a Coke) we tried the course again. I ran the Tornado for the first few laps and pushed the tach up into the red zone on the long back straightaway. I don't know exactly how fast I was moving, but it was enough to scare me. Without the visor, it would have burned the skin off my face.

"Is that your choice for the weekend?" Carl asked.

"I think so. I'm beginning to get the feel of it."

"That's a lot of bike. It was too much for Sam."

"I know."

The Tempest, I knew, was the right bike for those infield corners. But up on the main track? I could make up a lot of lost ground with the Tornado there. And I really was beginning to find communion with it. I would skip the Saturday lightweight, save it all for Sunday.

Dick Mann came over late that afternoon, as we were getting ready to load. "Hud tells me you boys are from Hardin."

We nodded.

"How's Sam Delgado doing these days?"

"He's eating," I said. "Two of these bikes are his."

"That's what I heard. You must be a comer. Sam doesn't make many mistakes."

"Thank you," I said.

"Rex is about the fifth or sixth best rider in Hardin," Carl explained, "and that's a very large metropolis."

Mann laughed. "I've seen it. Good luck, boys."

He went away and Carl asked, "Why'd he come over?"

"To be nice. The man's an immortal; he can afford to be nice."

"Was that irony or cynicism?"

"Neither. Quit yacking; I'm hungry. Let's go!"

I had talked face to face with Dick Mann, a hero more heroic than Monte Brand. The glow of it lasted through dinner.

Sunday's 200 was the big one at Daytona, but there were other races we entered that week. They were short-track races at Memorial Stadium, across town. I picked up a hundred and fifty dollars in these and Carl picked up experience. It wasn't a fortune, but it would buy a lot of hamburgers.

Through the week, I'd been wearing my old leathers. Sunday morning I put on the new outfit, a going-away present from Joe.

Carl stared at me, wordless for a change.

"Classy, right?" I said.

He nodded.

I showed him my new helmet, a present to myself, finished in metallic green lacquer, flecked with gold. "Let's go," he said.

There were even brighter colors out at the track, the red and white of Triumph, the orange, black, and white of Harley, the bright green of Kawasaki. The stands were filling; there would be close to sixty thousand spectators here today.

73

Carl had just missed qualifying; he would be my one-man pit crew. He tried to be cheerful but it was obvious his disappointment was deep. Under his bantering surface, he was as competitive as the rest of us—almost.

"You've turned some fast laps this week," he said.

"In practice, yes. Not in qualifying."

"You qualified. Play it cool. There are a lot of stormers here who are going to blow themselves out of it early."

I nodded. There was a tightness growing in me, a self-doubt. A few seconds slower, and I wouldn't have qualified.

From two pits away, Dorn came over to stare at me. "Man, where'd you get that outfit?"

"My fan club took up a collection."

"Sharp!" He expelled his breath. "Hot, isn't it?"

"It'll get hotter."

"For sure. I wish Jody was here. He brings out my best."

Jody calls it your worst, I thought. I said, "I wish he was, too."

"Take care," he said. "Let us not shame the glorious name of Hardin." He went back to his pit, where a local mechanic was fussing over his Harley.

There would be one mandatory pit stop. We planned to make it about halfway through the race, somewhere around the thirtieth lap, depending on my position at that stage. Carl had worked pits before; we wouldn't lose much time there.

Mann had won the lightweight on Saturday and come back to qualify for the pole in this one. Yours truly would start seventy-seventh in a field of eighty. Even a man walking could finish higher than that; the heat and the pace would narrow this field today.

Eighty big engines droned into life and swung down the the curve to the infield. At the tail end of the parade, the Tornado grumbled impatiently. She had probably expected to start in faster company than this. I had not served her well.

I tried not to be as impatient as she was. I was no charger; if I had any skill as a rider it was finesse. On the first turn in the infield, the rider ahead of me misjudged his pace and left the course. These things would happen this afternoon; in sixty-plus laps, they would happen often. Only the men in front were storming now, trying to find room to breathe and breeze.

We advanced three more positions before skidding through the hairpin and up onto all-out alley. The racket here must have been heard in Miami, big engines at full throttle, tires burning rubber the length of the track. Man, that Tornado could move! Bikes of all colors went sliding backward through the acrid smoke of burning oil. We picked up at least a dozen places in that spurt.

The tightness was still in me, but it was tension now, not uncertainty. I had the mount, that much was clear. And I really felt I had the moxie.

The confidence had come from the competition; I'd been running with the also-rans. The deeper we bored into that field, the tougher it got. In the seventh lap, we moved up on Mickey Dorn and took him, but it hadn't been easy. The uncertainty returned to the human half of this team. Nothing seemed to be troubling the Tornado; she did everything I asked of her. It was possible I wasn't asking enough.

On the twentieth lap, the slate in Carl's hands informed me we were running forty-second. We had moved up thirty-five places and found the company rough. The competition ahead was bound to be even rougher. There was a way to find out and the Tornado was willing. I twisted her higher.

The first name we closed in on was a big one, Bart Markel, a man who doesn't like to be passed. We passed him. I suppose it would be more honest to explain how. His machine was belching blue smoke at the time; he was heading for his pit.

When we pulled in for our pit stop at the thirty-second lap, we were in the upper third of our field. We hadn't passed that many bikes. The area around us was loaded with disabled machines. I was weary and aching and wind-burned; the next half shaped up as pure torture.

"Smooth," Carl told me, "very smooth. You're running twenty-sixth. Don't blow your cool."

Twelve seconds later, the tank was full and we were back into action. Carl Rowland could work a pit almost as well as he could talk.

I would need to finish in the top twenty to pick up any points at this meet. Easy enough, you might think—until you consider that these were the fastest bikes and the best riders in the world.

My road racing experience was limited. The Tornado was still not my favorite mount. I probably should have entered with the Tempest yesterday. But I was here and still running, better off than two-thirds of the boys who had started.

Play it cool? What else? As I've explained before, I was no charger and no stormer. I would race the way I knew best. Ahead of me, in the thirty-sixth lap, a hot-shoe from

Tulsa missed the third turn in the infield and we were finally in the top twenty. All of the riders had made pit stops by now; Carl's quickness there had gained me the other five places.

Twentieth place earned from 1 to 1.4 points, adjusted to the size of the purse. Earning only a point a meet was not the road to Number One, but this was not my kind of racing. Once we hit those dirt tracks. . . .

Losers' thoughts, Rex Smalley, quitters' thoughts.

Move, little man, the Tornado seemed to grumble. *These guys aren't that much better.*

I was moving faster than I had ever moved in my life on the ground. I had traveled further than I had ever traveled in a race. All of this for a possible maximum of 1.4 points?

What I didn't know at the time was that the leaders had tangled in the final hairpin and gone down. We were running eighteenth and moving up on the German champion, Boots Koch, riding a BMW. The modified frame housed a four-stroke, one-cylinder engine almost 600 cc.'s in displacement, transmitting its power through a driveshaft instead of a chain.

It was a finely engineered machine in the hands of a champion. My rookie arrogance and the Tornado's impatience were a luckier combination today. We edged by on the long stretch before the infield turnoff and zoomed into seventeenth place.

There were five cycles in sight now, five places a stormer might pick up in one lap—if he valued points more than his hope of seeing tomorrow.

Patience, little man; tomorrow is bound to be better than yesterday. We closed in on Italy's second-best rider, Vito

Martino, screeching a tight corner in his factory-tuned Benelli. There was no way to take him in the turn. We trailed him, inhaling his exhaust, all the way back to the main track before moving into sixteenth place.

Dreaming and thinking and hoping, they are all done above the neck, but they are not the same. I had dreamed of winning this, hoped to finish in the top third, thought I could finish still running. I was now riding better than the hope but short of the dream and almost sure of the thought. There were only twelve laps to go and no stutter of complaint from the Tornado.

Finishing sixteenth would earn between five and seven points. That wasn't much of a bulge to take out of a race this important, nor a comfortable start for the new season. From behind, Bart Markel was closing in, moving faster than a sensible man should. He blasted past with no argument from us. I had seen his cycle in the pits through three circuits; he couldn't possibly be running in the same lap.

He wasn't. The slate informed me we were still sixteenth as we droned past our pit, a quarter of a lap in front of the nearest challenger. Eleven laps to go. The ache that had started in my shoulder had worked down to my knees and up to a spot behind my eyes.

Unless the boys ahead had trouble, sixteenth was our best hope. The Tornado still had reserves; I had none. We were running as fast as I could safely handle this late in a race this long.

I take no credit for our advance in those last eleven laps. Credit the Tornado for her stamina. Credit the heat and the pace and luck. We were almost a full lap behind Hud Eggleton's Triumph when its engine seized and he went sliding sideways into the hairpin. He was running in a crowd at the time; he took three bikes down with him—and we rode twelfth.

Mark Brelsford's Harley threw a rod; Chuck Palmgren's Yamaha cracked a fork; Buzz Leftwich's Dormer blew a tire. There was no challenge left in me, only the ache and the bone-weary determination to keep moving. Beneath me, the Tornado continued to sing, carrying its spent rider into ninth place, two laps short of the checkered flag.

Somewhere in the middle of the infield, I think I heard her grumble, but there was no waver on the tach. The noise, the heat, the grind, the tension and the stink of castor-tinted carbon monoxide had left me subject to delusions. The Tornado was made of sterner stuff; she rode on, untroubled.

We held our pace; we held our place. We finished ninth in the big one at Speed Week in Daytona.

Chapter Eight

"Beautiful," Carl said. "Smart, cool, gutty—beautiful!"

"Thank you. Who won?"

"I don't know. Some guy from Finland with a name I can't pronounce. He was riding a Yamaha. The first three finishers were all riding Yamahas."

"A foreigner? On a Yamaha?"

"Foreigners, too, are people. What are you, a bigot?"

"You know I'm not. It's the first time, that's all. No foreigner has ever won *this* race before."

"One has now. Yamaha shouldn't surprise you. They've been winning here all week."

"Sure. But this was the big one. Harley and Triumph were really pointing for it this year."

"Too bad for them. But good for us privateers."

"How?"

"That Finn won't be traveling the circuit, so his points can't hurt us. You picked up twenty-eight points, tiger."

The noise was gone, the crowd was going, the seagulls were coming back to the infield. The tension was draining out of me, leaving only the ache and the weariness.

"Twenty-eight points," Carl repeated. "Smile!"

"I'm too tired. Let's get the trailer loaded. I think I've earned a fat steak and a long sleep."

The steak and the long sleep helped. In the morning, I was closer to normal and ready to relish my achievement. Five Yamahas, two Hondas, one Suzuki, one Triumph and the *only* Temple in the race had finished in the top ten. The Triumph had finished fourth, piloted by Dick Mann. He would carry eight times as many points as I would out of Daytona, but he was Dick Mann. He was the best—today.

Eleven of the first twenty finishers had been California riders. It was possible I had underrated the competition of my apprentice years.

"If you're through reading about yourself in the paper," Carl said, "finish your coffee. It's time to hit the road. We're a long way from the National at Louisville."

"We've got six days," I said. "I figured to pick up some traveling money in Georgia."

"Georgia? Where?"

"Gaspar. It's a half-mile track and they have Wednesday night races. Sam told me it's easy money."

"You won enough money this week. Louisville makes more sense, Rex. We can get to know the track."

"It's your camper," I said. "You're the boss."

"Don't pull that poor boy bit. Don't make me feel guilty. Okay, Gaspar it is. I hope the money's easy."

That's one of the things I'll never forget about Gaspar. Carl hadn't wanted to go; I had.

Gaspar was a county seat and the track was at the county fairgrounds. It had been a horse track and it was still banked as a horse track, shallow. It looked as if it hadn't been graded since the First World War.

"Sorry, now?" Carl asked, as we studied it on Tuesday.

"Not if they pay in cash."

Next to the leaning judges' stand, a couple of kids were bending over a Harley Rapido. We went to introduce ourselves.

"I've forgotten their names, but they knew mine. "Rex Smalley?" one of them said. "Didn't you just take a ninth at Daytona?"

"The exact same famous person," Carl answered for me. "My name is Rowland and I once took a third at Tucker's Grove."

The boys frowned doubtfully and said nothing.

"Getting ready for tomorrow night?" Carl asked.

They nodded. One of them said, "Aren't you going to Louisville?"

"That's where we're headed," Carl answered. "We thought we might pick up some eating money on the way."

"If you're light eaters, you might," one boy said. "The new promoter pays peanuts."

A new, cheap promoter and a track that could have qualified as a disaster area. Why did I stay?

82

"How old are you guys?" Carl asked.

"We're both fifteen," one of them said. "But I'll be sixteen next month."

Carl looked at me and back at them. "Where do we sign up?"

The taller boy said, "The man's name is Craddock. He runs the Magnolia Gas station in town. You can probably find him there."

It was a two-pump station of sheet metal, selling cut-rate gas and off-brand tires. The man named Craddock was tall and heavy. I had a feeling he should have been wearing a black hat.

"California, eh?" he said. "Seeing the country, are you?"

"More or less," Carl said. "Do you have an AMA sanction?"

"The man I bought the lease from had one and nobody's taken it away from me. So I guess I still have it. What are you boys running?"

"I'm running Hondas. My partner here finished ninth at Daytona on his Temple Sunday."

"I don't know much about Florida racing," Craddock said, "but ninth doesn't pay off at Gaspar."

"We'll try to do better here," Carl promised. "Do you have any entry forms?"

"There should be some around somewhere. Hold on; I've got a customer."

He went out to service the drive. Carl looked at me.

"My idea," I admitted, "and a bad one. Let's get back on the road."

Carl smiled and shook his head. "A dirt track and fifteen-year-old competitors? I need it for my ego. What can we lose?"

We ate lunch in the camper and drove back to the track. It was being dragged now, the brightest spot in the day so far, and there was a roller waiting for the dragging to be finished.

The two boys were gone. At the far end of the pits from us, a man about thirty was easing a Suzuki down a homemade ramp from the bed of a pickup truck.

"Shall we go over and yack with him?" Carl asked.

"I think I'll take a nap. Wake me when the man's finished with the roller."

"Rest in peace. I'll go over and get the word."

I was passing Dick Mann in the last lap at Ontario. Joe and Jody were watching from the pit; Mom and Lisa were watching from their box seats. Suddenly, the Tornado began to sputter and shake beneath me. . . .

It wasn't the Tornado that was shaking; it was my shoulder under the hand of Carl. "Wake up, King. The track's ready."

"How long did I sleep?"

"Almost two hours."

"Learn anything?"

"It's not all kids, I learned that. And they draw pretty good crowds. Some of the riders come down from Tennessee, and the fans come from all around the county."

"Maybe it wasn't a total loss. Have you tried the track?"

"Not yet. I didn't want any unfair advantage."

I put on my old leathers and went out to unload the Tempest. There were five of us here now; the boys with the Harley had returned.

"You lead, I'll follow," Carl said. "If you go down, I'll know where the soft spots are."

I didn't find any spots softer than the rest of the track. It was like riding through water. We made two circuits at the speed of a trotting horse and pulled in.

"I thought Georgia was clay country," I said. "If that's clay, you're a mute."

"I think it's a combination of loose sand, feathers, and peat moss," Carl said. "We'll never get to know it sitting here."

"Maybe the Trail Cat would work better."

"You could try it."

I tried it and it was better. Not good, just better. It delivered less torque but found more traction and I could muscle it around these soft turns better.

By four o'clock, there were seven or eight riders practicing, and the surface was again as rough as when we'd first seen it. It isn't my nature to anticipate catastrophe, but I couldn't shake an uneasy feeling about that track.

"There's no groove," Carl complained.

"Our best groove is the road out of town."

"We're here," he said, "and we're entered. Think we could find any real southern cooking around here anywhere?"

"There's a place called the Dixie Café in town."

He shook his head. "That sounds like greasy meat loaf to me. I'll ask my new friend with the Suzuki."

The restaurant we went to was in Eudora, a town about twelve miles away. It wasn't exactly gourmet cooking, by Carl's standards. It was southern fried chicken and candied yams, a lot tastier than camper cooking, by my standards.

My stomach was now contented but the uneasiness persisted in my mind. I would go with the Trail Cat all the way tomorrow night. There would be both lightweight and open qualifying sprints with separate finales.

We worked on our bikes in the morning and tried the track in the afternoon. It had been sprinkled, dragged, and rolled again while we were working. It was still a dangerous track.

"Don't look so gloomy," Carl said. "I've been clocking a few of the boys and their laps aren't any faster than yours."

"Did you clock yourself? I have a hunch *your* laps are getting to be faster than mine."

He laughed. "It's possible. Maybe this is all I ever needed for success—a bad track."

It was all he needed for what happened. What happened couldn't be called success.

The track was closed to practice at four o'clock. We had an early dinner but didn't get back until about seven. The pits were jammed with cycles now, the stands already half full. The lights weren't the best, but they were better than I'd expected.

"Wednesday night," Carl said. "It doesn't figure, unless they work a two-day week around here."

"They race on Sundays, too. Haven't you been reading the *Gaspar Gazette*?"

"I tried. I guess I didn't get to the ads. Which qualifying sprint are you in?"

"The second."

"I'm in the first. I was hoping I could prove my superiority."

He didn't prove complete superiority; two cycles finished in front of him. But he proved his excellence, moving up from ninth place through heavy traffic to finish only fifty feet behind the winner.

"Another lap," I told him, "and I think you would have won it."

He nodded.

"You qualified, though."

"Yup." He climbed off his bike.

"You're kind of quiet, Windy."

"I'm kind of shaky," he explained. "These boys play rough. Be very careful out there."

I had seen the action and I had planned to do just that. On a track I could read, I was no more subject to intimidation than any other rider. On a track this treacherous and this far from home, caution was a wiser course than bravado. I didn't carry many extra parts for the Trail Cat; I carried no extra parts for myself.

That was the attitude I took into the qualifier. It might have been responsible for what happened.

A short race on a bad track doesn't allow a man space or time for clever strategy or patience. The aggressive riders I competed against fought for advantage in the very first turn, throwing up a cloud of dirt as thick and frightening as a desert sandstorm. My view ahead was as unsure as the ground beneath the Trail Cat's tires. You can say I chickened out; my estimate of it is kinder. Frankly, it was no place for me. Bart Markel, maybe, Jody, Mickey Dorn. Not Rex Smalley, not this night, or any other.

There were twenty-one entries in the heat; we finished seventeenth. If four riders hadn't gone down, we would have finished twenty-first. We had not qualified for the lightweight windup.

Carl stared at me when I came in, but said nothing.

"Thank you," I said.

"For what?"

"For saying nothing."

"What's there to say?"

"There's nothing to say. But I can't remember that it's ever stopped you before."

He shook his head. "Man, you're sour!"

"I'm sorry," I said. "I guess I'm a bad loser."

"When did you first notice?" He turned his back on me and walked over to his bike.

I followed him over. "I apologize, Carl. I really am sorry."

He still had his back to me. "Okay, okay! Apology received and accepted. One item for the record, though—I wasn't the one who wanted to come here."

"I know."

He turned and smiled. "Now let's talk about me and my imminent success in the lightweight finale."

"I wish you every success in the world," I said. "I hope you come out of it alive."

It was a twenty-bike field and a twenty-lap race. I was almost glad I wasn't in it. Many of the riders were young, and all of them made up in fervor what they lacked in skill. Carl combined enough of both to move from seventh to fourth place in three laps, his Honda perking sweetly, finding traction where none was visible.

He used a lot of track but kept gaining ground. It was

a smart and gutty show, the best performance I had ever seen from Carl Rowland in competition.

He made his big bid in the twelfth lap. He was running third behind a pair of Tennessee brothers wheeling Harleys. They were evidently favorites at the track, greeted wildly by the fans every time they passed the stands.

Carl kept moving up and should have taken them both. That is an objective, not a subjective opinion. Carl was better and his bike was faster.

The lights weren't bright enough nor the air clear enough for me to see exactly what happened in the backstretch of the thirteenth lap. Through the haze and the dust, I could see the Honda closing in and moving wide. From where I stood, I couldn't see whether it hit a soft spot in the track or a ridge or if there had been a collision. I could see the bike go end for end and Carl flying through the air.

I started running across the infield as the ambulance pulled out from its space next to the judges' stand. . . .

Chapter Nine

The county hospital was about a mile north of Gaspar. I met Mr. Rowland in the waiting room Thursday morning. He had taken a plane to Atlanta and a bus from there.

"No worse than you told me on the phone?" he asked.

"No worse. His right leg is broken, two ribs are cracked. The doctor just told me he's doing well."

"Have you seen Carl this morning?"

I shook my head.

"Can I see him now?"

I nodded. "Room 212."

"Come along," he said.

Carl was sitting up in bed, his leg in a cast. He was reading a paperback novel. He looked up and stared at his father. "No hollering, please, Dad."

90

"Not now. I'm glad you're alive. I'll holler later. Are you feeling all right, son?"

"I'm feeling lucky. It could have been worse."

"I'm well aware of that. Carl, I have a plan."

Carl waited, saying nothing.

"I'll stay around until you're ready to travel, and then we'll go home together in the camper. We can see the country. We can get to know each other, maybe."

Carl smiled. "You planned a two thousand mile lecture?"

"Nothing of the sort. Try not to be facetious. Don't you want to do it?"

"I really wish we could, Dad," Carl said, "but Rex needs the camper."

"No!" I said. "I won't use your camper, Carl. I'll buy a used truck. I've already looked at one."

"*Where* did you look at one?"

"Craddock's got an old Chev panel in pretty fair shape for three hundred bucks. I intend to buy it. There's no way I'll use your camper."

"Okay, tiger, okay. Thank you." He looked at his father. "Give me the lecture now, Dad, while I'm sedated, and we'll save the good talk for the trip home."

I left them there, a father and his son, and went back to the Magnolia Gas station to dicker with Craddock. He wanted three hundred; I offered him two hundred. We settled at two-fifty and I had transportation, so called, for my continued quest of Number One.

I never saw Louisville. The diaphragm in the fuel pump ruptured twelve miles short of Chattanooga. By the time I could get help and a new fuel pump, the race at Louisville was out of reach. I headed northeast, toward the next championship point event, the twelve-mile, dirt-track National at Reading, Pennsylvania.

That old Chev panel didn't purr like Carl's camper, and I missed his bright chatter. We clanked on, a legal orphan in an alien land. This was the trail that led to the Grail. Who needed company? I did, but I wasn't ready to admit it.

I had bought a sleeping bag in West Virginia; the panel truck was now my transportation, my garage, and my home. I washed in filling stations and ate in cheap restaurants, preserving capital.

I ran both the Tempest and the Tornado at Reading, with pit help supplied by a Philadelphia Temple dealer. I didn't hurt his business any, picking up points, picking up enough money to squander on a motel room that night, and my first shower in a week.

The famous names on their factory mounts had been there. But I had finished third in the lightweight and fifth in the open class. Some of my confidence was back, some of my loneliness gone.

The next circuit stop was in Phoenix, too far away for my purse or my truck. The point event after that would be at Riveredge, up in Massachusetts, two weeks from now. I drove over into New Jersey, to a town called Cannister, to pick up some travel money.

The track was the same length as Tucker's Grove, a third of a mile. It looked harder and was banked higher. Except for the open space in front of the stands, it was surrounded by a high board fence, only a foot or so from the upper edge of the track. There was no way to slide off the rim without crashing through the fence. It was spotted with new lumber.

92

Nobody I knew was there, not a single California rider. There were cheap lodgings available, but they didn't look as clean as my sleeping bag; I slept in the truck.

At a pizza parlor about a block from the track, I got the word from the counterman. There were two night races a week, Friday and Sunday. The man to see was Tony Miratti. I could find him in his office behind the hot dog stand near Gate Three.

Mr. Miratti was short, dark, and narrow, matching his office. "Didn't you take a ninth at Daytona?" he asked. "You finished pretty high at Reading, too, if I remember right."

I nodded. "Gaspar was my downfall."

"Never heard of it," he said. "We don't get many California riders here."

"I noticed that yesterday. There were some fast bikes working out, though."

"Good boys, too. But I don't pay appearance money."

"I never met any promoter who did," I said. "I'm looking for hamburger money."

"That's about what I pay," he admitted, "depending on the gate." He paused. "Most of my riders are local. They kind of gang up on strangers. If they box you, don't make it personal."

"I can't promise that."

He shrugged. "Okay. It's your neck. The track's open for practice, if you want to try it."

I signed the entry form and drove across the track to the gate that led to the infield. There were about a half a dozen riders in the pits, two out trying the track.

Watching yesterday's practice, the cycles had looked fast

93

to me. I knew why after my first lap on the Tempest. This dirt was as hard as macadam and offered better traction. Combined with the steep bank, that made it a fast track, the fastest short track that I had ever ridden.

Centrifugal force was the big problem here; a man could easily be lured into taking those steep turns too fast. There was a reason for the board fence. I ran about ten laps and came in.

It would be all lightweight, Amateur and Junior-Expert heats and finals. It might be Rex Smalley against the field, too; nobody in the pits came over with a word of greeting. I worked on the Tempest and tried a dozen more laps and then drove over to a trailer court about half a mile away.

There was a public shower here and a laundromat, a counter restaurant within walking distance. I showered and washed my dirty clothes and tried to nap in the truck, but I couldn't. I kept remembering those men in the pits.

I went out into the murky Jersey sunlight and noticed we had a new tenant. A Volkswagen van with Oklahoma plates was parked in the stall across the way. A blond kid with hair down to his shoulders was tinkering with a Yamaha DS7 in the narrow space beside the van.

He saw me watching him and waved. I went over.

"Georgia plates," he explained. "You must be here for the racing. Why else would a man come to Cannister?"

"I bought the truck in Georgia. I'm from California. My name is Rex Smalley."

He frowned. "Smalley? That name rings a bell. My name is Gary Voltz."

"How can you miss?" I said. "A lucky name and a winning bike."

94

"Come again?"

"Gary Nixon, Gary Scott, Gary Fisher—all winners. And Yamaha sure cleaned up at Daytona."

"That's it!" he said. "Daytona. You ran there, didn't you? How'd you finish?"

"Ninth in the two hundred. Were you there?"

He nodded. "Watching, not racing. Didn't you run a Temple?"

"Right."

"Ninth," he said. "Ninth in the big one! Could I buy you a beer?"

"I never touch it. It might stunt my growth. You could buy me a Coke. There's a machine in the laundromat."

He was nineteen. He'd had two years at Oklahoma State and no further interest in formal education. "This country's sick," he explained. "I wanted to get a good look at it before it dies."

"It's been sick before," I argued. "An Okie should know."

"If you're talking about the Depression, our national health reached an all-time high. Poor isn't sick. Rich, that's sick."

"Let's not argue," I said. "I need all the friends I can find in this town."

He laughed. "You must have been out to the track."

"Right."

"Provincial bunch, aren't they?"

"I guess that's the word."

He smiled. "I was lucky I had my hair under my helmet. I think I'll buy a net for it before Friday night."

"You're big enough to wear your hair down to your knees," I said. "They didn't scare you, did they?"

"One on one, nobody scares me. But Miratti told me these boys gang up."

"Well, there's two of us now. At least one and a half. And there must be some more out-of-state riders on the way."

"Let's hope so. Are you hungry?"

"I'm always hungry. Put up your hair and I'll buy you your dinner."

We ate at a Chinese restaurant on the other side of town. He was an interesting talker, though not up to Carl. He never really said it, but I got the idea his folks weren't hurting for money. The saddest thing about money is that the people who don't have it seem to be the only people who appreciate it.

"You don't talk much about yourself," he said.

"I'm the only American citizen born in Alkali Junction who ever took a ninth at Daytona. From this humble beginning, I hope to go on to even dizzier heights."

He laughed. "You're only half kidding, aren't you? Cycles, they're your whole world, aren't they?"

"Right now," I admitted. "Wouldn't you like to be Number One?"

"Nope. I race only when I need the money. This trip was *my* idea. I didn't think I should take it at my father's expense."

"Racing can't be the easiest way to make money on the road."

"It is for me. I'm very good at it."

"Man, you're humble!"

"Wait. You'll see."

I waited and I saw.

96

In the morning, we worked on our cycles. The timing on the Tempest had seemed late to me; Gary straightened it out in half an hour. Like Joe, he had a natural instinct about machines. I hoped his instinct about America wasn't as sound.

"That'll do it," he said. "Now I'll pin up my hair and we'll go over to see how they run. We might as well go together and save gas."

We went in the van. We were early. There was nobody in the pits or on the track. Mr. Miratti was standing in front of the refreshment stand, smoking a long, thin, black cigar. We waved, but he didn't wave back.

"He looks like a cut-rate mortician waiting for customers," Gary said. "If he pays by check, I'm going to cash it fast."

Enough Yamahas had finished ahead of me at Daytona and Reading to impress me with their quality. Not one of them had sounded any sweeter than that two-stroke of Gary's.

"You lead, I'll follow," he said. "Maybe you've discovered a better line than I have."

In the circuits I'd made, slightly above the middle of the track had seemed the fastest line, cutting the corners from there, finishing low. It was the route I took for almost three laps.

We were really winging when we pulled out of the grandstand turn on the third lap. But that Yamaha streaked past us like a meteor and I had a chance to study his line from behind, well behind.

It looked crazy to me, riding right to the peak of each

97

curve, then gunning down the slope into the straightaway, almost a V turn. He picked up a quarter of a lap on us before pulling into the pit.

"It's not like other dirt tracks," he explained, "where the upper third builds a soft ridge."

"It might build up in a race," I said, "when the traffic is heavier."

"I doubt it. Have you ever seen a dirt track this hard?"

"Never. But I don't think I could crowd that fence like you did."

He grinned. "Faint hearts don't win fast races."

"Some faint hearts finish first," I said. "I wouldn't want to cost Mr. Miratti any expense for new fencing. There's enough there now."

"Each to his own, Alkali Junction," he said lightly. "Let's go over and get a pizza. We've got all afternoon to practice."

He was young and a showboater, with no goal and not enough faith. But he was a mighty good man on a bike. If it had mattered to him, I think he could have become one of the great ones.

I tried to find a new strategy for Friday night between the line he'd shown me and the best of mine. A few more out-of-staters arrived on Friday afternoon, but we made no alliances. The locals had shown no hostility, only a continued indifference. Nevertheless, I remembered Mr. Miratti's warning when we lined up for the first five-lap, Junior-Expert heat.

I was in the third row, flanked by a bulky, bearded rider on a Harley, directly behind a rider with the same dimensions and facial foliage on another Harley. It looked like a

box. It could have been a coincidence. The starting positions had been determined by draw; if it was a box, the
track management had to be involved.

I never found out. The cycle on the pole sputtered just as
the green flap dropped and the rider in front of us didn't
react quickly enough, smashing into him from behind.

They both went down and we went wide, finding room
between them and our flanking bike because of the quicker
response of the Tempest. There were only two cycles in
front of us now, a Honda and a Kawasaki, running in tan-
dem, heading for the lower track. We moved past them
halfway through the first turn.

We were never headed. We were a hundred feet in front
of our nearest pursuer when we took the checkered flag.

"Fine work, faint heart," Gary said. "You finished first."

"I noticed. I think I was lucky."

"I think so, too. Those beavers on the Harleys looked like
brothers to me."

"How about you? What'd you draw?"

"I drew the pole," he said, "but that proves nothing.
Who fears me? I'm not famous."

He was in the second heat and the machines looked faster
to me. Right up to the green flag, they looked faster. After
that, they looked like they were running through molasses.
I had seen the best at their best; I had never seen any
better rider than Gary Voltz. It was a laugher for him.

"We ought to stay here all summer," he said. "We'd get
rich."

"And maybe crippled. Well, what can they do to us now?
They can't box us from behind."

"On a track this short in a ten-mile race they can. The

99

tail-enders can wait for us and do the dirty work when we try to lap them."

"That's pretty farfetched."

He shrugged. "It's happened before."

It happened that night, though I didn't even see the pattern of it until the twelfth lap. Gary was on the pole and I started next to him. His Yamaha jumped at the flag; I didn't accept the challenge. We both had clearance enough; I dropped behind, to let him set the pace.

In thirty laps, a lot could happen, and I wanted to check his line. It had been different in his qualifying heat from the line he'd shown me in practice. The upper rim V's had been rounded more, his down-slope charge had carried him further from the inner rail.

There were no problems from behind after the second lap and through the eighth. Gary led, we followed, the others trailed. We were dogging him closer than we had through the days of practice. My tach showed we weren't moving at the speeds he'd shown then. He was driving as fast as he had to. We could have passed him at this speed. It was too early.

In the ninth lap, the boys began to move closer. He must have noticed. The Yamaha took off, we followed, the gap behind stretched out once more as the Tempest's needle quivered near the red zone. The bikes were beginning to string out now; he was closing in on the laggards.

The bike running last was at least thirty feet behind the dueling pair in front of him. Gary tried to take him from the outside. He cut higher. So did the tail-ender.

Gary cut sharply toward the rail—and found himself in the pocket, behind the bearded man who had flanked me, pinned on the left by the rail, on his right by a lanky rider on a Suzuki. It had been a three-man play, the tail-ender the decoy.

Ahead, we had room in the scattered field and almost a full lap on all of them. We were in first place. But that was my friend in the box.

The Tempest complained as we slowed, but she knew who was boss. We had legal clearance for the rail and that was where I headed her.

The decoy was out of the action by then. The bulky man on the Harley slowed and tried to swing wide to go around us. It had been too abrupt; he forced his partner high. The gap was there, the Tempest spurted. Gary followed me out of the trap and we were off and running.

Two-thirds through the race, we had a lap and a half on the field, Gary trailing us by ten feet. We had been moving fast as I cared to, tonight—but ten feet? Never five, never fifteen, always ten? We slowed; the gap stayed the same. We moved faster and so did he.

I knew what he was doing. I didn't like it, but I took it, first place in the Junior-Expert windup on a Friday night in Cannister, New Jersey.

In the pit, I said, "You didn't fool me. Why didn't you make your move?"

"I'm moving," he said. "Coast to coast, north, south, east, and west. Besides, I owed you. It's my bread but it's your life. What do I have to prove?"

"That you're the best."

"I already know that," he said. "Let's load the bikes."

Chapter Ten

In the morning, we went to get our money. Mr. Miratti was in his office with his cigar and the *Racing Form*.

"I figured you boys would stay over," he said. "The fans liked you. I figured to pay you after tomorrow night's action."

"We're simple country boys, Mr. Miratti," Gary explained, "and we're leary about being outslickered if we hung around. We'll take our money now."

Mr. Miratti frowned. "I wasn't prepared for this."

"Could I use your phone," Gary asked, "to call my uncle in Westerville, Ohio? I'll pay the charges."

"Westerville, Ohio? Isn't that the AMA headquarters?"

"Precisely," Gary said. "They sure take a dim view of

hippodroming down there in Westerville. We'd like our money in cash."

Outside, I asked him, "Do you really have an uncle in Westerville?"

"None I know of. Most of my uncles are in Tulsa. Rex, it was a pleasure meeting you. Maybe we'll meet again."

"Aren't you going to Riveredge for the National?"

"Not this year. I want to take a look at Niagara Falls. Have you ever seen it?"

I shook my head.

"You should," he smiled, "before it's too late. I hope you get that Number One before you realize it's not important. Good-bye."

I shook his hand and he went his way. I went mine, neither sadder nor wiser. Maybe he was right. Who knows who's right? It's a free country, all opinions acceptable.

Through downstate New York and a corner of Connecticut, the panel rumbled along, the only noise coming from the engine, none from the cab. No jokes, no arguments, no observations (pro and con) on the passing landscape. So what? Wasn't I a loner?

In Springfield, Massachusetts, I bought two retreaded tires and had the oil changed. At a trailer park in Riveredge, I was consuming a wrinkled hot dog surrounded by a stale bun when Mickey Dorn's van pulled in.

"What happened to Carl?" he wanted to know.

"He broke a leg and cracked a couple of ribs at Gaspar. His dad came to get him."

"Gaspar? Where's that?"

"In Georgia."

"Never heard of it."

"You're lucky. How come you didn't make Reading?"

"I went to Phoenix. I couldn't squeeze 'em both in. You did all right at Reading, didn't you?"

"Not as well as Nixon or Mann or Eggleton."

Mickey laughed. "Nothing personal, Rex, but you ain't them—yet!"

I'm closer than you are, I thought. I asked, "Why Phoenix instead of Reading?"

"My sponsor's idea, not mine. He was vacationing there. Been over to the course yet?"

I shook my head.

"Let's try it this afternoon. I hear it's *mean!*"

That was scenic country around Riveredge and so was the course, but Mickey had heard right, it was *mean.* The water was more creek than river, but it was as wet as a river, and we had to cross it four times. The shallowest places got the most traffic; the banks were already rutted and slippery as ice. I tried to find better traction on alternate crossings our second time around on the Trail Cat.

It wasn't only the water; there were some tight turns between very thick trees with very rough bark and a few slopes that could keep a cycle airborne almost long enough to require a flight plan from the Civil Aeronautics Board.

Mickey was running a Harley Sprint. We had no trouble staying with him. The Trail Cat had found her natural terrain.

The scrutineers were still checking cycles in the inspection area when we quit for the day. There were some high-point riders standing around and yacking while they waited for their bikes to be qualified for practice.

"Winners," Mickey said. "Every place you look, winners! Doesn't it get you down, Gabby?"

"Who wants to race against losers?" I asked. "We could have stayed in Hardin, if that's what we wanted."

"I guess I'm out of my natural atmosphere." He smiled. "I'm aching to go home and beat Jody again."

"You two should be friends," I said.

"We are—but Jody won't admit it."

There'd been no water in those desert scrambles I'd entered, and the few T.T. races at Ascot had been that in name only. Racing on a course with natural hazards, with jumps and water and trees, was new to me. For some reason, my confidence stayed healthy.

My practice laps were up there with the fastest; the gearing in the Cat seemed to be exactly right for this course. My time trial put us in the second wave. We would start five seconds behind the leaders.

The cycles were bright, the helmets glistened. Thirty-three laps from now, we would all be mud-gray and so would our bikes. Thirty-three laps from now, two-thirds of this field would be out of the running, either down or mechanically disabled.

We droned around a high outcropping of granite and started the winding, downhill trail toward the trees. We were second in our group of six. Nobody from behind challenged. The bike ahead gunned up to join the first wave. We followed.

In my practice rounds, I had tried to judge the passing areas as safe, dangerous, or impossible. There were more impossible places than safe places; there were more dangerous places than the other two combined. Most of the

105

track was a mixture of dirt, grass, and gravel, with two asphalt stretches where a rider could shift to top gear. I would need to stretch my limit of calculated risk.

The rider ahead was a kid from New Hampshire I had met at the trailer court. He was wheeling a Kawasaki. I had followed him in practice rounds and admired his strategy; I let him set the pace in the early going.

He was a great advance man, keeping us free of the pack behind, within sight of the leaders ahead. For four rounds, we moved without strain, riding eighth to his seventh.

The traffic from the rear moved closer in the fifth round and my pacesetter reacted with a bad move, crossing the stream at a shorter, but deeper, point. His ignition washed out. From here in, my strategy would be my own.

A Honda crowded us on the left as we came out of the water and into a tight, slippery turn before the first stretch of asphalt. The Cat's traction was better; we beat the Honda to the hard surface by five feet and never saw it again.

Two tail-enders of the first wave were still in sight on the asphalt. We were pressing them before I had to downshift for the wide turn back to the trail. Again, the Cat's traction was better. We took them both on the inside and started up the hill.

I will never get used to being airborne on a cycle. There's no sense of control in the air, no comforting feel of surface against tire, of being the master of the machine. But we hit the peak of the hill at full throttle.

We almost blew it right there. Correction—*I* almost blew it right there (I hadn't consulted the Cat). In our practice runs, I had hit the crest slower, giving me plenty of landing room to brake for the sharp corner that led back to the

106

forest. As we soared today, I had the scary feeling that we were headed for downtown Boston.

There was a hummock of granite guarding the inner edge of the turn below; there was some mighty soft and treacherous ground on the other side of it. Beyond it was a tree. Between soft ground and a hard tree, the choice for survival seemed to favor the ground.

It was the choice I made, knowing our speed would be too much for that soft surface, hoping that after we went down, both the bike and I would still be able to operate.

I had a few yards of road left for braking as we landed, and I used every screeching inch of it before we swerved into the soft ground. The Cat shuddered as if she'd run into a tidal wave. She shuddered and shook and complained— and went on. Through the field, back to the trail, she ploughed, my new favorite Temple machine.

Running fifth now, running well, between the tall trees, along the wide trail, no bike in sight, front or rear, though I could hear the bark of a dozen of them and smell the lingering exhaust fumes of the four in front.

Running fifth only because we had qualified high and there hadn't been many cycles to pass. But that, too, is strategy, qualifying high, and I might have been feeling smug.

Humility returned soon enough. Behind, the posse was gaining. Ahead, Bart Markel blocked the road to fourth place. As you must know by now, Bart Markel doesn't like to be passed. And to be passed by a rookie on a Temple? *He* was a Harley team ace.

I dogged him, too young and too dumb to realize the depth of my arrogance. He, too, had judged the places where it was safest to pass. He saved his best effort and his most dangerous speeds for those places. We went splashing through the stream and streaking through the dust, two mud-caked maniacs on overworked machines.

The dirt ovals were his favorite battlegrounds, as they were mine. He had been Number One three times, but he had scored the most points on the oval tracks; he was almost unbeatable there. Here, today, he might be better than I was, but he was not unbeatable, even by a trail rookie on a Temple. We took him on the highest hill of the nineteenth lap and rode into fourth place.

The three leaders were in sight as we hit the second stretch of asphalt. They stayed in sight for five laps, getting bigger every lap. Mark Brelsford, another Harley team rider, Gary Nixon on a borrowed Yamaha, and some eastern rider whose name I have forgotten—those were the three in front of this Hardin greenie on his Temple.

They were better than I was that day, probably. I mean Brelsford and Nixon, not the man I have forgotten. The big difference was the Cat. She had found a course to her liking; she made me look better than I was, that day.

We took Brelsford on the inside of the sweeping curve before the starting area. The eastern rider had forced him high and there was room; we took them both at the same time.

Which left only Nixon. *Only?* He had been Number One twice, a feisty little man, brave and skilled, with a background almost as hungry as mine. He was a Triumph team man, but they let him switch in lightweight events, having no lightweight machines of their own.

108

He was better than I was, and wheeling a Yamaha. Only one bike in the world could have taken him on that course that day and I was riding it.

We passed him short of the second crossing on the thirty-first lap and came out of the water with a solid advantage. Which grew and grew and grew. . . .

In one Sunday afternoon, at Riveredge, Massachusetts, I had tripled my point count for the year.

The photographers wanted to take my picture with the cup in both hands, but I convinced them the Cat deserved better than that. So they shot me standing next to her, and I made sure the big "Temple" on the tank was clearly visible. Two of them were wire service photographers.

At the trailer court, Mickey was out in front of his van, waiting for me. "Congratulations!" he said. "The kid from New Hampshire just told me you won."

"Thank you. What happened to you? Weren't you around at the end?"

"I wasn't around after the second lap. Cracked a cylinder, hitting the water, and I was too sour to stay and watch the rest of you guys have fun."

"Would a steak sweeten you? I'll buy."

"It might help. You picked up a bundle, huh?"

"Enough for a while. I've got another idea."

He waited.

"That fancy motel on the edge of town," I explained. "A double would cost only about three dollars more than a single. If you don't want to be beholden to a punk, you could pay the three dollars. We can get our steaks at the same place."

109

He looked doubtful.

"Their beds are bound to be softer than a foam rubber pad on a van floor," I reminded him.

"I accept," he said. "Pride is the weakest of my virtues."

After dinner, I put in a long distance call to Sam to relate the good news.

"I know," he said. "I've been trying to get in touch with you. I wanted to tell you you're even better than I thought. And you know I always thought you were pretty good."

"It was the cycle," I said. "Horses for courses."

"Daytona, too? And Reading?"

"I didn't win there. Is Carl home yet?"

"Yes." A silence. "Gaspar, that was my idea, wasn't it?"

"Don't look back," I said. "You'll never get as rich as your pa, looking back."

"Okay, Texas. Do you realize you jumped from twenty-eighth to seventh on the point count today?"

"I knew I jumped, but not *that* high!"

"Sleep on it," he said. "Pleasant dreams. Call me from Columbus if the news is good."

There were no dreams; I was bushed. In the morning, Mickey asked, "Columbus next?"

I nodded.

"Do you want to follow me, or have me follow you? I could save money and sleep better, bunking double."

"You'd lose at least one day of practice," I told him. "You'd have to drive in second gear to stay behind that heap of mine. I'll see you there."

There are many towns in America called Columbus, natch. This Columbus was in Ohio, the capital city of Ohio. Through the narrowest part of New York, through the widest part of Pennsylvania and a sliver of West Virginia, I traveled. Nineteen words can cover that distance in print. You should try it in a wheezing panel truck sold to you by a cut-rate gasoline dealer.

The clutch started to slip at a traffic light in Harrisburg. It could go at any time, I knew. If it wore out before we reached Columbus, I would have to buy another truck. There was no way a transient could get a new clutch installed in time to make the meet.

I nursed it; we made it.

Formerly a half-mile track, it was now a full mile of dirt, firm enough for traction, loose enough to slide a curve. Riveredge had bolstered my confidence. I might not be the equal of these stars; the Cat had been the edge. But I now knew I was good enough to be in their company.

I guess they did, too. Quite a few of them stopped at the pit to congratulate me and talk about the Temple line.

"Maybe I should have listened to Sam," Hud said.

"It's not too late. He's still talking."

"And I'm signed up. Well, the season is far from over."

True, true, true. . . . I was the seventh most successful rider on the circuit that afternoon—but the season was far from over. The worst part of it would start today.

The mechanic Temple sent over from the local dealer could have been a good excuse, if I had deserved one. I've forgotten his name, a fat man with a cigarette constantly hanging from one corner of his mouth, a fat man with a poor touch. He knew less about the machines than I did, but I should have known more. I'd spent enough years under Joe Milgram's roof to learn more.

We were swamped in the heavyweight and finished

111

eighteenth in the lightweight, thanks to my ignorance. I slept in the truck that night, cold and unhappy, and moved to a cheap hotel for the next two nights, while the truck was getting a new clutch.

"She needs a valve job," the service manager told me, when I went to pick it up.

He was telling me something I knew. I paid the bill and headed her toward Texas. It was far away, but there'd be time. The next National was twelve days from now, at San Antonio.

Ohio had been cold. Indiana was warm, and Arkansas steaming.

"Very unusual weather," the man at the filling station in Little Rock informed me. "It's generally nice this time of the year."

"We get a lot of it in California, too," I admitted.

"Nice, you mean? Or hot?"

"Unusual. How far is the track from here?"

"Track? Oh, you must mean Bernard Park. It's not much of a track." He gave me directions.

He had spoken the truth; it wasn't much of a track, three-eighths of a mile long, with a shallow bank and gaps in the fences. It would be night racing and all lightweight. With luck, I could pick up a few dollars.

I worked on the Tempest all day and brought it back to worse than it was when we had left Hardin, better than it was when we had left Columbus.

It wasn't right, but this wasn't Columbus. I picked up a hundred and forty dollars, racing against locals, on Saturday night, and headed for San Antonio.

Most of the stars who had been at Columbus were here

112

with their well-tuned cycles. They didn't need Cannister or Little Rock or Gaspar to keep going. They were here, well fed, rested, and ready to roll.

Don't make it personal little loner; they earned their places.

Gary Nixon stopped at the pit. "Why the long face, Texas? Bad news?"

I shook my head. "Just envy, I guess. I don't have to tell you. You've been where I am."

"And now I'm where you're heading. You've got it, Rex, and you probably know it. Any way I can help?"

"Nope. I'm still eating. Thank you, though."

"Sure. What happened at Columbus? The word I get from the California boys, that should have been your kind of track."

"It was. But my cycles were too slow and the company too fast."

He grinned. "Not for long, Rex, not for long. See you."

Any way I can help? Yes, Gary Nixon, Mark Brelsford, Dick Mann, Hud Eggleston and company, you can help. Slow down a little, so Crybaby Smalley can catch you.

Another voice, another face, Mickey Dorn's. He had gone down at Columbus; he was still limping. "I've had it," he told me. "This is my last show on this circuit."

"Running out of money or out of steam?"

"Ambition," he said. "Is it always this hot in Texas?"

"Not in the winter. Where have you been since Columbus?"

"Missouri. Town called Trellis. Picked up eighty bucks." He took a breath of the hot air. "Any message for the folks in Hardin?"

113

"Tell 'em I'm still trying. Tell 'em I'll be home when I'm broke."

I did better at San Antonio than I had at Columbus for one reason, again, the Cat. It was a hundred-and-fifty-mile race over a rocky, twisting, three-mile course. The Cat had been tinkered with the least since leaving Hardin; she still had the remnants of the Joe Milgram touch. We finished twelfth and picked up nine points. It didn't improve my state of mind.

Daytona, Reading, and Riveredge had spoiled me. Looking back on it now, twelfth in that field on terrain that was new to me had been higher than a sensible rookie had a right to expect. When a man's in a fog of self-pity, his values get distorted.

Alkali Junction wasn't too far from here. But what was there for me? There's no way now I can recapture the mood that made a trip to my birthplace suddenly important.

It was a hot trip in a limping truck through dull country to a dead town. What could I find there? How could it help my mood?

I think I knew but wouldn't admit it. Mrs. Adelaide Baskerville was there, the woman who had sheltered this loner, the woman who had persisted until she had found me a home. Maybe, at that stage, I wasn't ready to admit my debts. If that makes me a creep in your mind, remember this: I went.

A few things had changed, none for the better. The Rialto was showing an X-rated movie, the Alamo Café had a new Hollywood-type neon sign. The truck rattled on, toward the Home for the Homeless.

In the front lawn, the gray grass was knee-high. The sign

114

over the porch dangled from one rusty hanger. The place was deserted, all its windows broken.

An aged Mexican was sitting on the front steps, eating his lunch from a paper bag.

He didn't speak English and I didn't speak Spanish, but eventually he understood. He looked sad and he pointed, and I knew what he meant and where.

It was a small tombstone in a dreary cemetery on a quiet hill. It read:

ADELAIDE BASKERVILLE

1896–1973

God sent her

God took her away

I finally had a decent reason for crying.

Chapter Eleven

I'm not going to linger over the details of the trip after that. This is a story, not a dirge. The happiest day of the second half was at Indianapolis, where we took a third and picked up a hundred points. The unhappiest day was at Nazareth, Pennsylvania, a day with no points and no sense of fitness to be in this company. Fourteen hours later, I started for home.

This was the middle of September. There were still two point races in California, closing out the season, one at Ascot, the other at Ontario. I could still finish in the top five—if I won them both. My chances of doing that were as remote as the furthest star.

When the truck finally coughed its last, south of Chicago, two-thirds of my remaining capital went for a nine-year-old

Ford pickup with a noisy differential. When the differential gave up the ghost in Albuquerque, the quest was finished.

I put in the new differential, with help from a filling station mechanic, and we made it all the way home. We picked up sixty dollars in a short-track meet in a town called Doom, in Arizona. The Tempest was operating at about seventy percent efficiency by that time, but it was enough for the competition at Doom.

The early afternoon we drove up the blacktop drive between the green dichondra, my mood was mixed, but the dominant half was bright. It was good to be home, if you don't mind the cliché. If you do, read somebody else.

Mom was in the kitchen, baking, as usual. She turned and saw me and started crying even before she hugged me.

"My wanderer," she said. "My nonwriter, my baby boy!"

"I wrote, Mom. I wrote a lot, for me!"

"You wrote. About what? Races and money and points. Is that writing?"

"What else do I know, Mom?"

"Yes," she said sadly. "Sit down. There's some meat loaf still warm from lunch. You lost weight, didn't you?"

"A little. How's everybody?"

"Sassy and healthy, thanks to my cooking. I suppose you've been living on hot dogs."

"Mostly, since Carl left me. Is he still going with Lisa?"

She nodded. "They're talking marriage."

I said nothing. She said nothing. Finally, I asked, "And what does Jody think of that?"

She sniffed.

"He's stubborn," I said.

"The pot," she said, "is now talking about the kettle."

"We're brothers," I admitted, "more brothers than some brothers I've met. But nice kids, both of us, right?"

"As far as men go, yes."

I laughed. "Hey, Joe was right! That old Harley did liberate you. You're finally a women's libber."

"You and your memory," she said.

Another silence.

"What is it, Mom?" I asked. "Is it Carl that bothers you, or Jody's attitude?"

"It's all mixed up. Do you like him, Rex?"

"I do. He's not exactly our kind of people, but I like him." I paused. "We can trust Lisa's instincts. She's a very bright girl, Mom. Nothing personal, but I think she's smarter than any of us."

"Present company excepted." She put the meat loaf in front of me and some hot rolls. "All right, tell me about the points and the races and the money."

"I have almost seventeen dollars. I think I finished twenty-second in the point count. And now I'm home."

"And next spring Jody goes," she said.

I said nothing.

I'd had a shower and put on clean clothes and was trying to unsnarl a shoelace when Jody came to the room.

"Brother," he said, standing there, studying me. Then, "Welcome home." And then he came over to hug me, which is some display from Jody.

"I blew it, brother," I said. "I hope you do better."

He shook his head. "I'll settle for twenty-second, any time."

I laughed. "That'll be the day! Who won at Ontario?"

"Hud Eggleton."

"That makes him Number One for the year."

"Right. Remember what he told us at Phoenix last fall? No more trail for him, he said."

"It gets in the blood. How have you been doing?"

"Fair enough. You and Dorn weren't around, but I found some other pigeons I could beat. Wasn't any of it fun, Rex?"

"A lot of it was. And all of it did me good. It's hard to explain. Maybe it's a fever. You know what I mean better than I can tell it."

"Sure," he said. "Sure. Oh, it's good to see you!"

Two more hugs, Joe and Lisa, some tears from Lisa and we were back to where we'd been in March, only better. Lower-middle-class living in a California stucco cottage. Seem humdrum to you? I liked it.

Back to the rubbish truck, a shiny new GMC, back to the local tracks, back to the cycles tuned by Joe. I liked it, but the fever was still in my blood. Irrational? Sure. What kind of fever is rational?

At dinner one night, I told Joe what Gary Voltz had told me, about being Number One not being important.

"Who am I to argue with a smart college kid?" he said.

I said nothing, smiling, waiting.

"Why the smile?" he asked.

"I'm waiting for the argument you're not going to give me."

"Okay. Any time you are the best in the world at what you do, I think that's important, if the trade is honest. He must like bikes, or he wouldn't ride one. Maybe he thinks he's the best in the world and maybe he is—but there's a way to prove it."

119

"Maybe he thinks that's carrying competition too far."

"Maybe. And maybe he doesn't want to test himself. He must be a good kid, if you liked him. I'm not going to rap a man who isn't here."

"Maybe, maybe, maybe, maybe!" Lisa said. "Is that what racing is all about?"

"No, bright and beautiful daughter," Joe said, "that is *exactly* what racing is *not* about."

"Racing!" she said. "Phooey!"

"Insurance!" Jody said. "Double phooey!"

That's what Carl was doing now, an insurance broker with his father's firm. Lisa's blue eyes could have burned through carbon steel. "Easy, brother! Be *very* careful!"

He was. He shut his mouth. Even hothead Jody knew when he was overmatched.

Gus Heinrich had finally gone first class and applied for an AMA sanction for Tucker's Grove. So points earned there now counted toward both rider advancement and the regional ratings.

Racing, as Joe had said, is not maybe. The points were there for any man to challenge, the fairly judged record of achievement. We worked days that winter and raced nights and weekends at the western tracks.

In December, Sam left a message for me to drop in at his agency after work. I knew what he wanted to talk about and I knew what I'd have to tell him, but I went over just the same.

"I talked with Mr. Melchior by phone this morning," he told me.

Peter Melchior was the president and majority stockholder of American Temple. I said nothing.

"He admits you helped sales," Sam went on. "I guess he'd have to. I doubled mine, after Daytona. But I couldn't sell him on the idea of financing a factory team."

"Even if he did, I couldn't be on it. We talked about this a month ago, Sam. Jody goes next year. I run the business."

"You've been way ahead of Jody on the western point standings all fall."

"That has nothing to do with it."

"It has for me. Melchior won't back a team, but he'll back *you*. Temple will put up most of the money. I'll put up the rest. You can go out this time with a chance to really prove yourself."

"Prove what? That I'm financed?"

"Prove that you're as good as the other winners when you're well prepared."

I shook my head. "It wasn't money I needed, the last half of the season. It was a sharp mechanic."

"Like Joe?"

I nodded.

"He'll go," Sam said. "I've talked with him."

I stared at him. "He never mentioned it to me!"

"How could he—without telling Jody, too?"

"He can't," I said, "and I don't want him to. Jody and I had an agreement and it's still binding."

"I'll talk with Jody."

"No, you won't. You say one word about this to Jody and I'll never say another word to you the rest of your life."

Sam's exasperation was deep and it was in his voice. "I don't understand you. I don't understand you, *at all!*"

"That's because you've never been an orphan," I said.

121

Our winter rains made the gray hills green. They also made the rubbish wet and the tracks gooey. We hauled the rubbish so we could eat and ate so we could race.

At the San Valdesto hundred miler in January, there were six stars entered, exactly six riders high in the National count. I know, because Jody counted them.

"I figure to finish seventh," he said.

"With your mouth. In your mind, first. It could be eighth. I'm here."

"Sure. But you're my brother. You wouldn't shame me in front of all these winners, would you?"

"You didn't show me any pity at Oxnard." He'd had a great day at Oxnard, winning easily.

He grinned. "I'd forgotten you were there. You were there, weren't you?"

I had finished ninth. "I don't remember," I said.

His grin went away. "You know you're good enough for these boys, Rex. But today could be a test, for me."

His mind and his mouth were in tune now. A determined Jody on a long, loose track against the big boys—the thought of it made me nervous.

What do you say? You say the cliché. "Easy does it," I said.

With Markel and Eggleton, Brelsford and Mann, easy does it? No way. And easy had never done it for Jody; it wasn't his way to go and he didn't.

He and Markel, those were the stormers this track was designed for, riders who take it personally when you challenge them. They had the fans hoarse a quarter of the way through the race. The rest of us could have sat in the stands, too, for all the competition we gave that pair of cowboys.

There would be one pit stop for gas; Jody made his the first time he had a clear advantage over Markel. He lost the lead when he went in, but he lost it by very little. When Markel went in, nine laps later, Jody's lead ballooned to half a lap.

Some other riders might have breezed. Not Jody. Any rider who tried to breeze with only a half-lap lead on Bart Markel had a lot to learn about his trade. Jody set a new track record for one lap in the eighty-second lap. He broke his own record in the eighty-third.

Mann and Eggleton were third and fourth. We trailed them. They were the best of friends, which made them the fiercest of adversaries. They would extend their sense of calculated risk eventually, affecting their sense of traction. And there would be room for cunning Rex Smalley to sneak past below.

We took them in the eighty-seventh lap. We now rode third, only half a lap behind Markel, a full lap behind Jody. He knew I wasn't pressing him; he would certainly remember lapping me. He was only a hundred feet in front of us. We made no move.

Nobody in the world was going to pick up a full lap on Jody in thirteen laps, not that afternoon. We were in the ninety-sixth lap, Jody in the ninety-seventh, when we saw Markel's Harley lying in the ridged dust of the south turn and Bart standing wearily by the upper fence.

Jody had it in the bag now. Yours truly seemed a cinch for second place. Nobody challenged us and I didn't challenge Jody. In his present state of mind, I was leary of the response even a lapped challenger might trigger.

He was a mile and a half from the checkered flag when

it happened. His Honda sputtered, wavered, and slowed. We went wide and past, into first place, where we finished, two and a half laps later.

There was gloom in our pit. There was gloom in the cab of the truck, going home. There was gloom and a silence as heavy as stone.

In our room, he sat on his bed, saying nothing. Finally, "I'm really stupid, don't you think?"

I shook my head. "So you made your pit stop a couple laps too early. It looked like a smart move at the time. It was the best edge you'd had on Bart up to then."

"That's stupid," he said. "Bad strategy is stupid. I made the pit stop too early—and that's why I ran out of gas. I'm not going to Daytona, Rex. I'll run the business."

"No," I said. "Tomorrow, we'll talk about it. Or next week. Not now. It's not the time to talk about it now."

"Yes it is. Today wasn't the decider. You think I can't count? You think I haven't been watching you since you came home? You're better, Rex. And what you told me that first day we walked to school together, that's true."

"Told you—? What?"

"You don't run out of gas."

Chapter Twelve

Traveling with Joe was different. Not that traveling with Carl hadn't been fun; don't read me wrong. Traveling with Carl had been an adventure, leaving home, which all young men do, eventually. With Joe, I wasn't leaving. Where Joe was, that was home to me.

And it's fair to say I was traveling with a fan instead of a critic. A fan is better for the ego. Building the ego helps to give a man the confidence (or arrogance?) he needs for National Trail competition. Add Joe's wrench to the above and it's clear I was better prepared this spring.

But there's a lot of ground between twenty-second place and Number One. Being better prepared might not be enough. Most of the winners were well prepared; it still focused down to the man in the saddle. That remnant of my loner philosophy stayed with me.

There had been almost as much tire failure as mechanical failure at Daytona last year, the high bank speeds burning rubber like an incinerator. A slowing chicane had been inserted in the backstretch. It was still enough track to frighten Joe.

"It's no place for cycles," he said. "It wasn't designed for cycles."

"Scary, isn't it?"

"Crazy!" he said. "And you're going to run it twice."

We were entered in two classes this year, the Saturday hundred, the Sunday two hundred. Last year had been a Yamaha picnic. Their competitors had spent the winter planning revenge. Some hot newcomers had been signed by factory teams to add to their monopoly of the veteran stars. There would be a sprinkling of Temple riders, all privateers.

In the cafeteria, the stars sat with us, this year. We weren't the magnet; Hud Eggleton had joined our table.

"Surprised to see *you here!*" he said, grinning.

"Surprised you can recognize me from the front," I said. "I guess you know Joe."

"I guess I do. I wish I had him."

Bart Markel laughed. "You could advance a number, Hud. From one to zero. But you'll probably make it without help."

Hud sighed. "The envy of inferiors—"

Sarcastic banter, back and forth around the big table. Why is it men insult each other only when they like each other? I'd have to ask Mom, the women's libber.

126

My awe of these men was gone, but not my wary respect. Most of them were friendly, between races. Out there, in the arena, competition soured and steeled them. Professionals can't afford friends when they're working. A few of them confused competition with war.

Yamaha had taken eight of the first ten places in the lightweight last year. Their ace, Gary Fisher, was back with a new model this year. He and Mann had to be the favorites on Saturday.

They were the early pacesetters, setting too fast a pace for most of the field. The veterans didn't try to match it. The hot newcomers who did were soon out of it, burning up their engines under the Florida sun.

A different Gary was my pacesetter—Nixon. He, too, was riding the new Yamaha, and the piercing whine of its two-stroke engine made my head throb. I stayed behind him, a man who rode this course well, who could teach me by example.

In the twelfth lap, we were running eighth and ninth, the Yamaha whining, the Tempest barking, the air fouling, the tension building. On the longest stretch, Gary stepped up the pace, a hundred and thirty-five pounds of wire and fire, looking for giants to topple.

We followed. I had taken him at Riveredge on the Cat. This was another day, another race, another mount. I would need to be better than I had been at Riveredge to take him today.

The test never came. In the fourteenth lap, a tail-ender he was lapping had an engine seizure and Gary had to leave the course to avoid crashing into him. A rider must reenter

127

the course at the same spot he left it. By the time he could get turned around, we were in eighth place and pulling away.

There isn't anything exciting left to relate. Except for one challenge, the only cycles we passed were either disabled or being lapped. The rider I challenged was Don Castro on a Yamaha. He was riding fourth at the time; he had finished second in this race last year. We were eight laps from the finish; we pressed him for three before he took a turn too wide and left a gap.

We were riding fourth with five laps to go. We finished third only because Bob Deiss' Harley had blown a tire two miles from the flag. Hud Eggleton won it on a Kawasaki; Ron Pierce took second. I had earned a hundred points, Hud a hundred and fifty.

"I'm proud of you," Joe said.

"It's mutual," I said. "Did Hud win it?"

He nodded.

"He's the man to beat, this year," I said.

Joe smiled. "Based on this race or last year?"

"Neither. Based on a four-year observation of him from the rear. He's got it all together, finally."

Tomorrow would be expert only and the points could be higher, adjusted to the prize money. Tomorrow, Hud would be running a factory Triumph, a machine he understood better than his mount of today. Last year's winner, Jarno Saarinen, the Finn, had been killed at Monza. Yamaha had no replacement to match *him*.

At the cafeteria table, Markel said, "Congratulations, Hud."

128

"Call me Mr. Zero," Hud said. "Where'd you finish, Bart, or did you?"

Bart smiled. "Almost. Wait'll I get you on the dirt!"

Hud yawned. "If I don't need the points, I might skip those meets."

"Why not skip tomorrow," Mann advised him, "and preserve your arrogance?"

Talk, just talk. They knew, as I did, that when hard-luck Hud Eggleton had become good-luck Hud Eggleton last season, his record really matched his skill. He had the cycles now, the mechanics, and the financial backing, all supplied by Triumph. His unlucky privateer days were behind him.

Two other Tempests had finished in the top twenty; there would be Tornados entered here tomorrow. The big one would be tomorrow, the climax of Speed Week. I had been here before, but I still didn't sleep well. Those big bikes and that fast track—Joe was right, it was a deadly combination.

There was an early threat of rain that disappeared by mid-morning. The overcast remained; today should be cooler than yesterday. For the sixty-three thousand spectators, that is. There was no chance the competition would be cooler.

Fisher and Mann had been my cofavorites yesterday. Neither had finished in the first ten. With that record, I made no prophecy for Sunday. I would guess only that the best man would win and hope his last name would be Smalley.

My time trial had been slow. We started in the middle of the field. Carl had been right last year; a lot of stormers would blow themselves out of this early. It still applied. We

129

were a long way from the checkered flag. Patience seemed to be the wise, early strategy.

Patience can be overdone. It was a cool day in Daytona and the engines were holding up. We gained only five places in ten laps, passing seven, being passed by two. My urge to move faster was strong, my conditioning of patience was stronger.

It began to pay off after the pit stop. We passed nobody in the thirty-fourth lap—but picked up three places. Cool and cautious now, Rex Smalley. Remember that everybody out here (but you!) is wearing a black hat. They don't put on their white hats until the race is over.

When the sun came out from behind the overcast, the temperature in the strained engines rose with the temperature of the air. No cycle here was cooled better than the Tornado; attrition became our ally.

Let me modestly summarize: we finished fourth, behind Brelsford, Nixon, and Mann, in that order. Let me add, before putting on my white hat, we finished three places ahead of Hud Eggleton.

The camper we traveled in and the trailer hooked to it had been bought second-hand by Sam from an insurance agent named Carl Rowland. Joe drove and sang country songs in his twangy baritone; I watched the road unwinding, the road to Louisville.

"This is the life, huh, Ace?" Joe asked.

"So far. If you get tired, I'll drive."

Joe shook his head. "Driving this monster could make you heavy-handed. Do concert pianists lay bricks?"

"I don't know. I haven't met as many concert pianists as you have."

"Traveling with Carl sure sharpened your tongue. I wonder if he and Jody are talking to each other by now?"

"Carl always talks," I said. "The hard part is getting Jody to listen."

"Ain't that the truth? He'd better learn soon."

"Don't rap my brother. Should we stop in Nashville and buy you a guitar?"

"With a voice like mine, who needs a guitar? A file, maybe, or some sandpaper. But I sure don't need a *gee*-tar!"

He had scratched and scrambled and brought up three kids. Now, for the first time, he was on the road and doing what he wanted to do. A family man, don't get me wrong. But it's not only women who need to be liberated.

Louisville won't go into my treasure chest of favorite memories. The Tempest was perking; I wasn't. It could have been the fatigue still lingering from those endless blistering laps at Daytona. Why alibi? It wasn't shameful. We took forty points out of Louisville, only ten less than Eggleton.

We came back a little at Reading, earning twenty points more than Hud, but fifty less than Nixon, who won. All of the boys were cutting into the pie; it would be no one-man banquet for Hud.

Phoenix was scheduled for later in the season this year; we headed for Riveredge.

"Pretty country," Joe commented.

"Until you see the course. My high point last year."

"I know. That Cat's the best engineered bike Temple makes. Do they have different engineers for different models?"

"I know as much about that as I do about concert pianists. It wasn't exactly a winner at Gaspar."

131

It wasn't exactly a winner at Riveredge, either, not this year. Dormer had come up with a modified off-road machine for Hud, hoping to lure him from Triumph. There were a few riders who complained it violated the AMA factory stock allowances, but the scrutineers didn't agree. He beat us to the flag by twenty feet and thirty points.

"Shenanigans!" Joe said.

I shook my head. "Those scrutineers don't make many mistakes."

"One's too many, and they made it today. Should we file a protest?"

"Joe! Are we whiners?"

"If a whine makes us winners, why not?"

"Joe!"

He grinned. "Of course we're not going to protest. I was testing you. I wanted to make sure I brought you up right."

Columbus was a high point this season. At Columbus, Rex Smalley (temporarily) became Number One for the first time in his limited history.

"It's about time," Joe said. "I suppose Eggleton will have that hot Dormer at San Antonio."

"You can bet on it."

I would have lost the bet. Nixon had taken possession of *that* Dormer under the AMA claiming rule at Riveredge. But Dormer, a new and aggressive company, had supplied Hud a twin of it for San Antonio.

Identical twins are not always equal twins, not after Gary's slick mechanics added their touch to his machine. He was in front of Hud from the green flag to the checkered. But there were two riders in front of Gary who stayed there.

132

Gene Romero won; we finished second, still Number One, halfway through the season.

Talladega, in Alabama, was hotter than Daytona and the speeds were faster. Tires would be the problem here. Tires designed for the infield turns would not be right for the bank. We settled on tires for the bank, rounded, almost treadless Dunlops, the same kind we had used on the Tornado for Daytona. The high bank, that was where the Tornado was designed to run.

That was where Gene Romero won it, building up his biggest advantage on the bank. That was where he took over Number One from your narrator. His Triumph led for all but a few of the two hundred miles. He was the first rider (and the last) in the season to win two consecutive Nationals. We finished fourth, Eggleton third.

There were five men now being chased by the posse, Romero, Smalley, Brelsford, Nixon, and Eggleton. Markel and Mann were the leading riders in the posse. With a little luck, they could become the chased instead of the chasers.

Markel joined the chased at Lakewood, in Atlanta. It was his kind of dirt and his kind of action. Brelsford moved down to join the chasers.

Most of us missed the hill climb in Pennsylvania and the short-track meet in Illinois, but not all of us. Markel picked up fifty points in the race at Hinsdale, moving ahead of me in the National count.

"This is murder," Joe said, on the road to Pocono.

"What is?"

"This race that never ends, this point count nonsense. A race should be a race, complete in itself."

"You sound like Gary Voltz. You should let your hair grow."

"Now, what does *that* mean?"

" 'Maybe he thinks he's the best in the world, and maybe he is, but there's a way to prove it.' "

"I wish," Joe said wearily, "you wouldn't quote me when I'm as tired as I am right now. Will you drive for a while? I'm going to try to get some sleep."

It might make me heavy-handed, I thought. "Sure," I said.

He tried to sleep and I drove toward Pocono. While I drove, I thought about my semifriendly adversaries. Eggleton had looked like the favorite, after Daytona, but Markel loomed as Mr. Big now. If he made it, he would be Number One for the fourth time in his career. Only one rider, Carroll Resweber, had ever accomplished that, back in the days when Harley-Davidson was undisputed king.

They were all good, maybe too good. I still had an edge; I had Joe and the Temples. The road unwound, Joe slept, the Temples rested.

There were riders living worse than we were, I knew, the privateers. But camper beds and camper cooking don't compare in comfort with stucco cottage living in Hardin. Even the few good restaurants we'd visited had no chefs like Mom. And Joe had a point; a race should be complete in itself.

I remember some of them the last third of the season, but I remember all the wrong things. I remember Hud blowing a tire at Pocono; Markel leading at Indianapolis—and going down in the dirt. Nixon tangled with Brelsford at Atlanta, taking them both out of it.

134

I was beginning to understand Gary Voltz. There are better things to see, traveling America, than the misfortune of your competitors.

Chapter Thirteen

We crossed the Colorado River at Blythe, just as we had, long ago.

"Cal-eye-forn-eye-ay!" Joe said. "God's country, at last!"

"Even the desert?"

"Even the desert. Even Los Angeles, in a way."

"What way?"

"Don't crowd me. I'm tired. Want to drive?"

"Sure. Do you think Hud has it wrapped up? He really came on, this month."

"Phooey!" Joe said. "We still have Ascot and Ontario. Who knows the blue groove at Ascot better than you? You were weaned at Ascot."

"And once saw a race at Ontario," I pointed out.

136

"You'll have time to practice there. We're home, son. Smile! Cheer up!"

"I lost my white hat," I explained.

"Whatever that means. Should I sing?"

"It might help."

He sang and I thought about fresh rolls and leftover meat loaf as the camper snaked along through the hot, dead desert, the trailer jiggling behind.

Jody was the only one at home, working in the garage on his big Honda.

"Pop," he said, "and Number Two!"

"Be kind," I said. "Where are Mom and Lisa?"

"Shopping. Rex, I meant that's great, Number Two. The season's not over. You ought to take Hud at Ascot."

I shrugged.

"You both look beat," he said. "Bad trip?"

"Tiring," Joe said. "Anything new to report?"

"Nothing exciting. I've been winning my share." He grinned at me. "Maybe I made the wrong decision after San Valdesto."

"Don't blame me. I tried to get you to reconsider. How's Carl?"

His grin remained. "Windy as ever. We get along, in a limited way. Let's not talk about him. Let's talk about the trail. I'm proud of you, brother."

"We can talk inside. I want some milk and a homemade roll."

Being home helped. My doubts didn't leave, but they were diminished. My own bed, Mom's cooking, Lisa's chatter, they all helped. Traveling this broad and varied country

137

with an open ear had softened some attitudes without destroying them. I still wanted to be Number One.

I knew Ascot, but so did Hud. There had been a National eight miler two years ago, a twenty-five lap T.T. race last year. This year, it would be a fifty-lap lightweight race, twenty-five miles of dust and chaos, with plenty of nontrail local riders to add spice.

Locals in Gaspar and Cannister are not the same as locals at Ascot, this record should indicate, by now. These locals were *good*.

Jody would not be one of them. He would be in the pit, along with his limited friend, Carl Rowland. They would be at Ontario, too. If we didn't do well at Ascot, Ontario might not be decisive. If Hud finished first at Ascot, Ontario would be meaningless.

Another of Jody's new limited friends, Mickey Dorn, came over to visit before the first qualifying heat Saturday night.

"You surprised me," he admitted. "You're better than I thought."

"Thank you. Still wheeling Harleys, I noticed. Still fooling the same sponsor?"

"Not really. His sales are up and I'm his biggest ad. Rex, I hope you make it. I like Hud. I guess I like you better."

Nice to know, but not as important as what he almost did for me later. He almost eliminated Hud in their qualifying heat, passing him in the last lap. A quarter of a lap from the flag, Hud was out of it—until two bikes collided in the grandstand turn.

He would start far back in the field and half-mile dirt

tracks were not his most successful battleground. We started in the first row.

Not all of the names were here, but Markel was and so was Romero. And the current Number One, of course. I never saw Hud, after the start. It was Markel who gave me the early trouble, and then his minor league twin, Mickey Dorn. I diced with Markel through the first twenty laps. The king of the dirt was determined this Number Two rookie should learn humility.

Another rookie, a kid from Bakersfield, was Markel's undoing. His Suzuki swung wide as Bart was passing him, taking them both out of the action.

We had been first or second through the opening twenty laps, trading places with Markel. We rode first through the next twenty. It wasn't exactly a breeze; there were a lot of young tigers here not impressed by National ratings.

We fought them off, one at a time, teaching them the humility Bart had tried to teach me. The Tempest seemed to take it more personally than I did, snarling and trembling over the churned dirt.

Ten laps to go and still leading; Ontario would have meaning. Ten laps to go, and my newest fan, Mickey Dorn, came up to have some fun. His idea of fun was different from mine, rubbing wheels, crowding from the inside. Intimidation, that was his idea of fun.

We're different, Rex, remember that. Don't play his game. Cool, cool, cool, now. . . .

The Tempest snarled, I held my temper—and the lead. Mickey's bulldozer strategy had lost him ground on the far turn of the forty-seventh lap, when he'd slid up the bank almost to the rim. With three laps to go, we were running first and free.

With two laps to go, we were not quite as free. Mickey's Harley was closing in. He challenged in the last lap.

Did my coolness lose it, or the sputter I thought I'd noticed in the Tempest in the backstretch? Why look for alibis? We lost it by the thickness of a tire to Mickey Dorn and his Harley.

We were ten points behind Hud Eggleton in the National count. Winning this would have put us back to Number One by twenty points. Hud hadn't finished.

"Dorn!" Jody said, and a few things unprintable. "Dorn *again!*"

I couldn't help it; I laughed. Carl laughed. Joe smiled.

"What's funny?" Jody demanded. "Are you all crazy?"

"We must be," I said. "Why else would we be here? Let's get her on the trailer. Mom's got a turkey roasting at home. We have to build up our strength for Ontario."

Ontario, the Daytona of the West. It was close enough so I could practice there and sleep at home. The format would be changed this year, one day of racing, open class, two hundred miles over a course slightly changed from last year. Run what you bring and hope for the best.

There was a piece in the *Times* by the cycle man. "Showdown at Ontario" was the head on his column. Only two riders, he explained, still had a chance for National Number One, and it would be resolved Sunday at Ontario. It looked like a promotional piece to me. Most items out of Los Angeles were and are.

I handed the paper to Jody.

140

"That's the way it is," he said, after reading it.

"A showdown? The Alkali Kid and Humble Hud in the dusty street in front of the saloon? It's a race, Jody. There'll be a hundred riders competing."

"Against you and Hud, mostly."

His jaw was set. I said, "I guess you're right."

Sam phoned that night. "Melchior's coming out from Akron for the race," he told me.

"Peter Melchior, the president of American Temple?"

"You know any other Melchiors? I think he wants to talk contract."

"*After* the race, I suppose."

"Well, probably. I plan to throw a party for him Sunday night. Most of the boys should be there. Keep yourself free."

"It's not easy. Will you be in the pit Sunday?"

"Not big Sam. I'll be in a fancy box with our esteemed president."

I would go with the Tornado. There had been some factory improvements in ignition which we'd added, along with the Dunlops. One pit stop for gas should be enough. The weatherman forecast heat and no breeze.

This had been a dream in spring, closer to reality now. It was not a tarnished dream, though it might have lost some luster. To be the best in the world at what you do, can that be unimportant? *Okay, Smalley, prove it and forget it, if you can.*

We were loading equipment in the dark Sunday morning when Joe said, "Gary Scott is a cinch for Number Three, isn't he?"

"Sewed up," I said. "What made you think of him?"

141

"I've been thinking of all the Garys on the trail. I started counting 'em until I ran out of fingers. That isn't what you'd call a common name, like Joe or Tom or Bill."

"Who was the big western star when they were born?"

Joe looked puzzled. Then, "Oh, sure! Gary Cooper! But they didn't name themselves."

"Nope," I said. "But there are fathers who like westerns, and even a few who like motorcycles."

He laughed. "Gary, Gary, Gary, Gary—all cowboys."

"Not Gary Voltz," I said. "Let's go."

Along the freeway we buzzed, toward the final rodeo at Ontario, toward the race *that* would make or break the season for me. I was beginning to think like that again. Who's perfect?

The race was hours away, the trials not yet started, but the immense stands were already a quarter full when we unloaded our equipment behind the pit.

The subject of our earlier discussion, Gary Scott, was in the next pit, gassing with his mechanics. "Sixty thousand miles," he was saying, "sixty thousand miles I traveled last year, just to make a living."

"Sixty thousand miles," one mech said, "to make forty-six thousand dollars. That's a pretty good living. And now you're a factory rider. That should make it easier."

"Who wants it easier?" Gary said. And then saw me. "Hey, Number Two!"

"Watch your language rookie. If you hadn't outfoxed me at Terre Haute and a few other places, I wouldn't even have to be here."

He grinned. "You'd be here."

Maybe, maybe not. . . . *Yes.*

It was a race. I liked to race. Forget Hud. Think of the race and think of the competition. If that bores you, Smalley, think of the money.

"Stop talking to yourself," Jody said. "It's almost time for your trial."

He and Carl pushed us to a start, and we swung down into the infield for the first step in today's strategy.

A lot of horse for such a light rider, but this course required a lot of horse. The prerace weariness I'd known so often on the trail was not in me today. I was ready and so was the Tornado.

Left and right, right and left, tight turns on tires not designed for tight turns. Up onto the main track, and those Dunlops paid off. The morning was already hot. I watched the tach carefully, not crowding the red. Smart strategy didn't demand starting in first place. More races are won late than early.

We didn't set any lap records. I hadn't tried to. We would start in twenty-ninth place, in the upper third of the field. The heat would be an ally, but Triumph had improved their cooling this year and Hud would be riding one. Engine size alone wouldn't guarantee stamina today. Those 350 cc. Yamahas at Daytona had outlasted engines twice their size.

In my Gaspar dream about Ontario, Mom and Lisa had been in a track-edge box. Not in reality. They were home, where they wanted to be.

Carl looked at the jammed stands and at me. He opened his mouth and closed it.

"A record," I said. "A new record."

143

"You? Today? You're planning to set a record?"

"Not me," I said. "You. You just set a personal record. You opened your mouth and didn't say anything."

"Stick with racing. I'll handle the humor. You're better than any of them, Rex. Go out and do it. Send 'em all back to Tucker's Grove, where they belong."

"Go!" said Joe and "Go!" said Jody and I went.

Into the infield, around the turns, under the hot California sun, competing with my peers. Another day, another race, but a good bed waiting at home and fine food.

Mr. Eggleton had told me two years ago that he would stay in the West and play in the sun. He had changed his mind about that. And today, under the western sun, he had qualified for the pole. Was that playing? It had looked like working to me, his Triumph burning up the course.

How can you burn and stay cool? How can you stay cool and take a burner? By letting him burn up, dum-dum. Two hundred miles ahead.

Attrition, my reliable ally, was still working, though not overtime. A few bikes went down, a few engines seized, some tires blew.

But not enough. At our (eight-second) pit stop, halfway through the race, we were running fifteenth.

"Fine!" said Joe. "Cool!" said Carl. Jody said nothing, frowning.

"Go," I said to the Tornado. "We can do better than this."

I said it on the high track, dogging Art Valeri, Pacific Coast point champion. We passed him in plenty of time to downshift for the infield. He seemed to be smiling. Art was not an Eggleton fan.

144

We were coming up behind the stragglers now, the tail end of the posse. They resented being lapped, and displayed it. The upper half of this team tried to show no resentment, only superiority.

Which prevailed. Fifteenth, fourteenth, thirteenth, the Tornado singing, the laps unreeling. Twelfth—and then eighth in one lap, one bike passed, three out of action. Attrition had gone into overtime.

Seventh, sixth, fifth. . . . The stink and the heat and the noise; I was glad Mom and Lisa weren't here to see, hear, and smell *this*.

Fourth, third. On an infield turn, the Tornado shivered and complained, and the Gaspar dream came back for a scary moment. But it had been the traction, not the engine; we went on, dogging Gary Scott, who rode second. On the dirt, many riders considered him as good as Markel. On any surface, he would be tomorrow's king.

He wasn't thinking about tomorrow. He was thinking about today. All of his friends were here; he was a local boy. We diced it out, *two* local boys.

There were three laps to go when we finally passed him. There were three laps to go and only Hud Eggleton in front of us.

Cool, now? With three laps to go? Attrition had punched the time clock and gone home. But hadn't I always played it cool and hadn't it brought me to where I was?

Another memory. . . . A kid with blond hair down to his shoulders, a kid who loved America and hated to see it die, a kid who'd told me, "Faint hearts don't win fast races."

Get ready, Hud. The sheriff's out of town and the citizens are depending on me. We'll meet in front of the saloon, in

145

the dusty street, before all these watching, waiting thousands at Ontario.

Two laps to go and we were close, close enough to challenge. Should we wait? Faint hearts don't win fast races. We took him on the long straightaway, an engine tuned by Joe better than any other cycle engine in the world. A biased opinion? I suppose.

We passed him and still had two laps to go and it might have been more sensible to lower the emotional temperature. But the Tornado wouldn't let me; Joe had given her a pep talk after I'd qualified.

I didn't even know where Hud was. I didn't learn until later that he had slid off an infield turn, trying to catch us, and been passed by Scott and Valeri.

What I knew was that I was the first to see the checkered flag. What I knew was that I was this year's National Number One. That was enough to know.

Sam was in the pit. Melchior had stayed in the box, talking business with some California dealers.

"Don't worry, champ," Sam said. "You'll meet him tonight, at the party."

"I won't be there," I said. "Not tonight. Bring him over to the house tomorrow, if he wants to talk contract."

He stared at me, wordless.

"Tomorrow," I repeated.

"Are you crazy? All the boys will be there! I wish I could understand you. I can't believe you're still a loner."

"That's just what I'm *not*," I explained. "Tomorrow will be soon enough for Melchior. Tonight, I want to spend with my family."

146

WILLIAM CAMPBELL GAULT has written more than two dozen sports books for young readers. Along with golf, horse racing, baseball, and football, he has covered auto racing in *Dim Thunder* and *The Checkered Flag,* hot rodding in *Speedway Challenge,* and sports car racing in *Road Race Rookie.* Mr. Gault lives in Santa Barbara, California, where he is an avid golfer when not busy writing.